"Planet X" Facts
Featuring Professor Twit & Roscoe

By
William Loyal Warren

"Planet X", Featuring Professor Twit & Roscoe

Copyright © 2024 William Loyal Warren.

All rights reserved. No part of this book may be used or reproduced by any means, graphic, electronic, or mechanical, including photocopying, recording, taping or by any information storage retrieval system without the written permission of the author except in the case of brief quotations embodied in critical articles and reviews.

iUniverse books may be ordered through booksellers or by contacting:

iUniverse
1663 Liberty Drive
Bloomington, IN 47403
www.iuniverse.com
844-349-9409

Because of the dynamic nature of the Internet, any web addresses or links contained in this book may have changed since publication and may no longer be valid. The views expressed in this work are solely those of the author and do not necessarily reflect the views of the publisher, and the publisher hereby disclaims any responsibility for them.

Any people depicted in stock imagery provided by Getty Images are models,
and such images are being used for illustrative purposes only.
Certain stock imagery © Getty Images.

ISBN: 978-1-6632-6491-6 (sc)
ISBN: 978-1-6632-6490-9 (e)

Library of Congress Control Number: 2024915434

Print information available on the last page.

iUniverse rev. date: 11/05/2024

Table of Contents

	Page
Professor Twit creates the robot dog, Roscoe	1
Professor Twit tests the mentality of Roscoe	2
Roscoe thinks he can do anything with his new programmed mind	3
Professor Twit introduces his assistants, Dr. Tamar and Dr. Newt to Roscoe	3
The debate of science verses religion goes on between Roscoe and Professor Twit	4
The infrared telescope is used by Professor Twit, Roscoe, Dr. Tamar and Dr. Newt	5
The discussion of our Milky Way and other galaxies in the universe	6
Roscoe views the travel of the earth through the Zodiac and the view of Pluto	7, 8
Professor Twit, Dr. Tamar & Dr. Newt discuss Planet X (Nibiru) with Roscoe	9
The illustration of the rectangle (Science, Religion, Fact and Fiction) is shown	10
Story about Sir Isaac Newton is told	11
How God's fingerprints are on the universe and our DNA	12
Calculation of the miles light travels in one light year	13
Illustration of the planets orbiting the Sun … and the Brown Dwarf Star	14
The various dates of Noah type floods, and the various Sun sizes in the Universe	15, 16
Definition of --- and Angel, Extraterrestrial Alien and a Demon	17
The size of our Milky Way Galaxy in light Years	18
Crashed UFO's throughout the world	19
Are Extraterrestrial Aliens nothing more than disguised demons	20
Picture of Angels, Demons and alleged Extraterrestrial Aliens	21
How fasting, charity and love exposes a disguised demon	22
The Ten Vibration Levels	23, 24
How the Armor of God protects and exposes one from demonic behavior	25
The infamous Black Holes in the universe	26
Review of material covered so far	27
The dangerous, life threatening chemicals to people and animals in the Chemtrails	28
Various kinds of stars in the universe	29
The use of scripture with astronomy	30
Fun Facts about the Sun	31
Fun Facts about Mercury	32
Fun Facts about Venus	33
Fun Facts about Earth	34
Fun Facts about Mars	35
Fun Facts about Jupiter	36
Fun Facts about Saturn	37
Fun Facts about Uranus	38
Fun Facts about Neptune	39

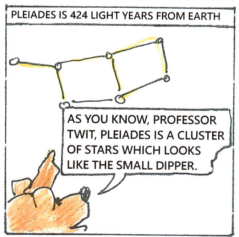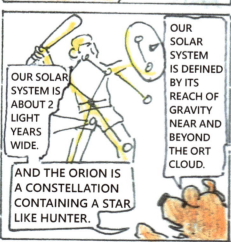

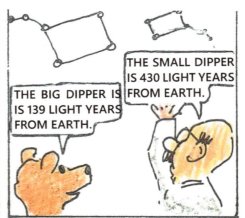

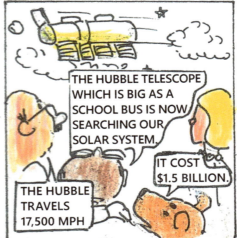

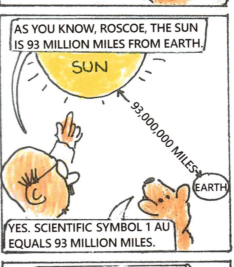

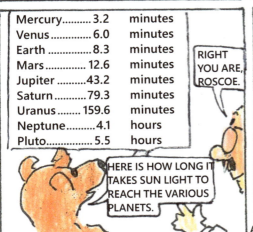

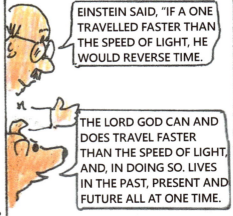

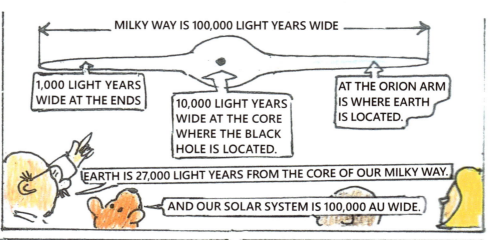
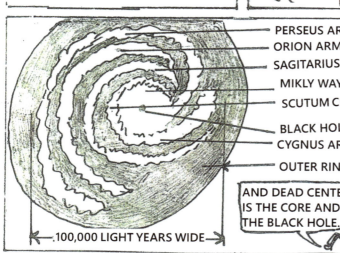
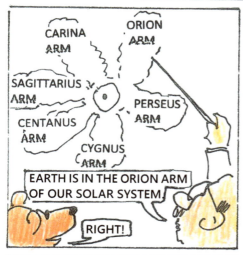
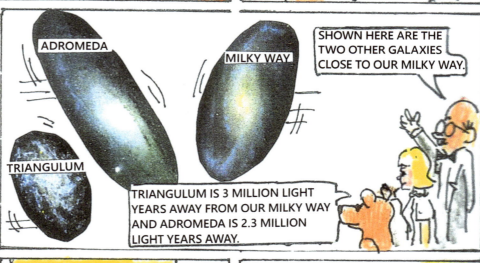

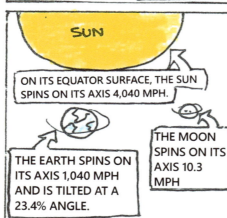
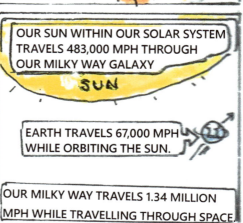

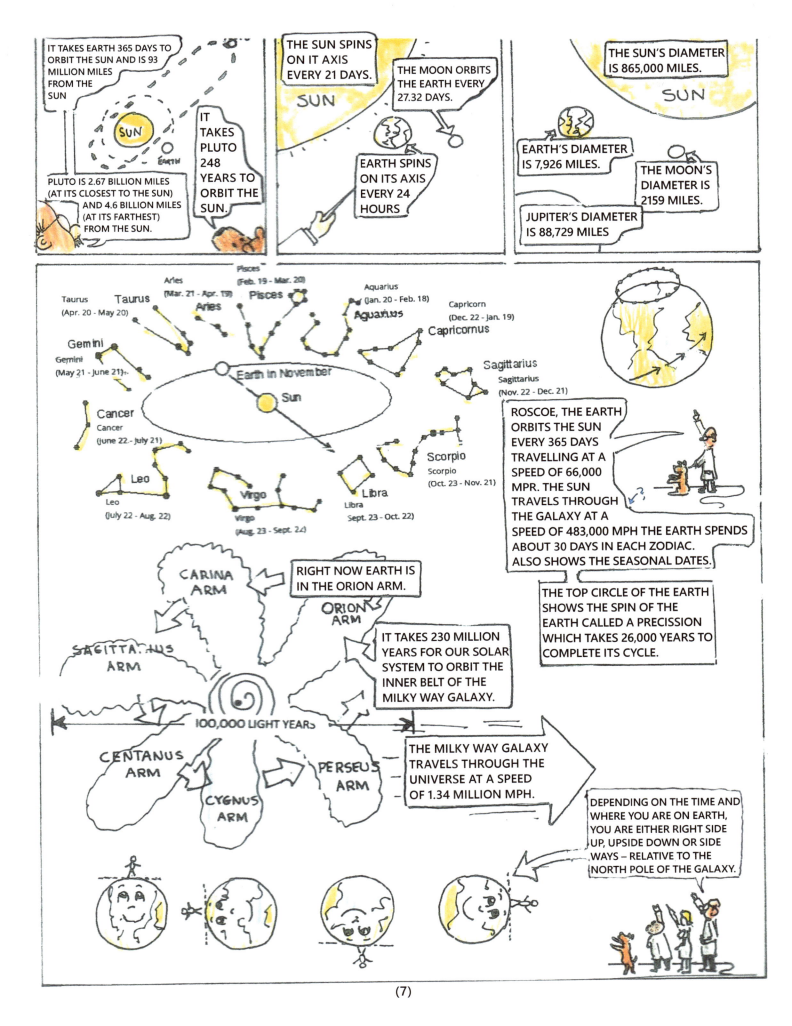

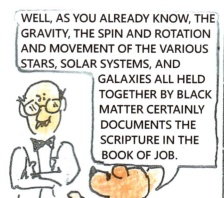

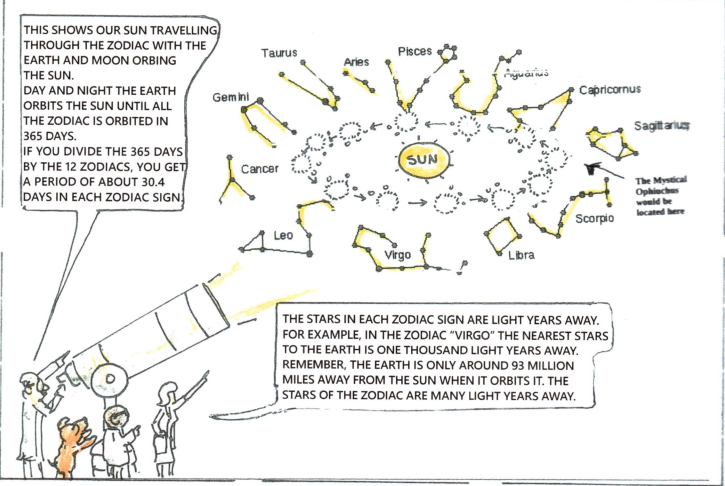
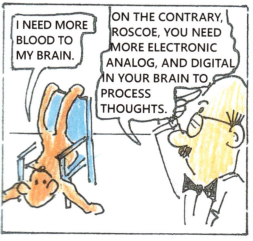

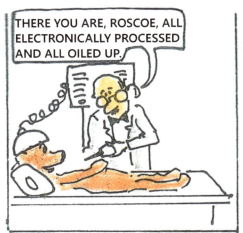

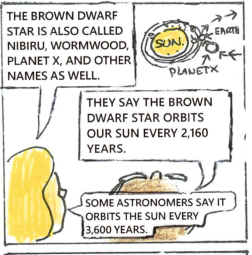

(10)

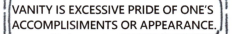

SIR ISAAC NEWTON STORY

(1) SIR ISAAC NEWTON ONCE HAD A MINIATURE MODEL OF THE SOLAR SYSTEM IN HIS OFFICE. THE SUN WAS POSITIONED IN THE CENTER OF THE MODEL WITH THE VARIOUS PLANETS DISPLAYED IN THE ORBIT AROUND IT.

(2) ONE DAY A FELLOW SCIENTIST WALKED INTO SIR ISAAC'S STUDY AND WHEN HE SAW THE SOLAR SYSTEM DISPLAY, HE EXCLAIMED, "MY WHAT AN EXQUISITE THING THAT IS. WHO MADE IT?"

(3) SIR ISAAC NEWTON REPLIED, NOBODY?"

(4) THE <u>SCIENTIST</u> LOOKED AMAZED AND SAID, "YOU MUST THINK I AM A FOOL OF COURSE SOMEBODY MADE IT AND HE IS A GENIUS."

(5) SIR ISAAC NEWTON LOOKED UP, SMILED AND EARNESTLY SAID, "THIS IS BUT A PUNY TOY IMITATION OF A MUCH GRANDEUR SYSTEM WHOSE LAWS YOU AND I KNOW. I AM NOT ABLE TO CONVINCE YOU THAT THIS MERE TOY IS WITHOUT A DESIGNER OR A MAKER --- YET YOU PROFESS TO BELIEVE THAT THE GREAT ORGINAL, FROM WHICH THIS TOY DESIGN IS TAKEN, HAS COME INTO BEING WITHOUT EITHER A DESIGNER OR A MAKER. NOW TELL ME, BY WHAT SORT OF REASONING DO YOU REACH SUCH AN INCONGRUOUS CONCLUSION.

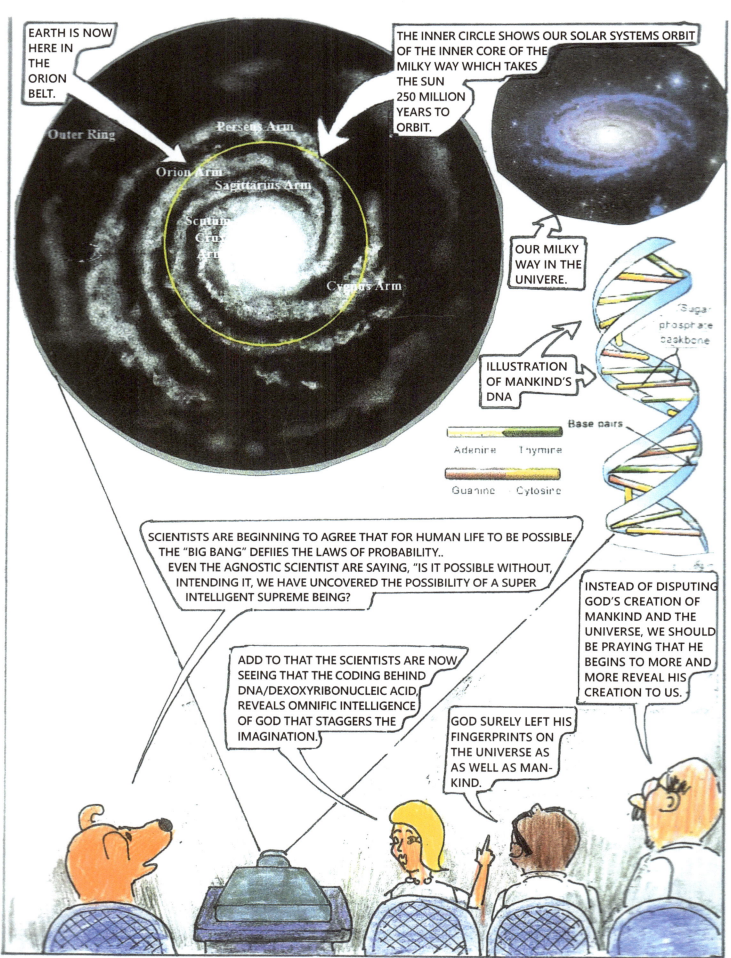

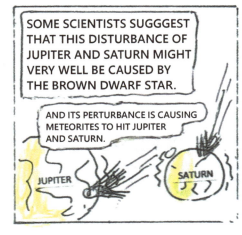

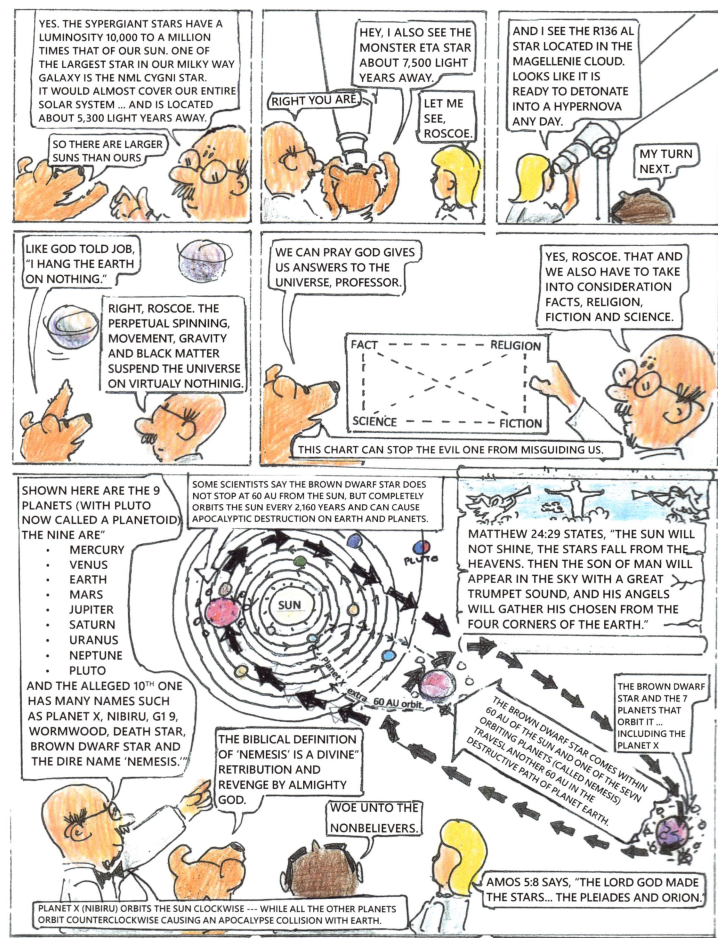

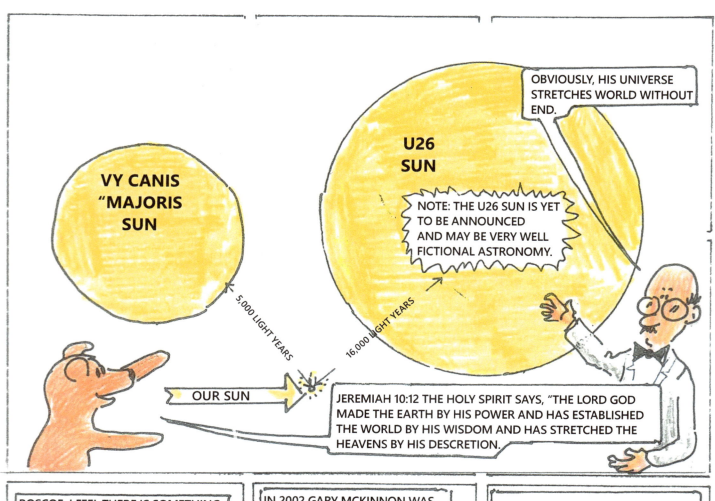
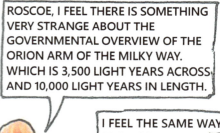

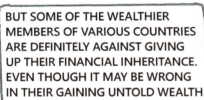

Panel 1: ACCORDING TO THE OTHER BOOK, 'EXO-VATICAN' THE ALIENS HAVE DIRECT CONTRACT WITH THE VATICAN.
BECAUSE OF THE JESUIT PRIESTS WORKING WITH THE INFRARED TELESCOPE IN ARIZONA..
MOST PROBABLY ... IF TRUE.

Panel 2: THE ALIENS, FROM WHAT I UNDERSTAND, WANT TO SET UP AN IFPS WHICH IS AN "INTERNATIONAL FUNCTIONAL SERVICE PLAN" TO TEACH NATIONS TO COMMUNICATE, PLAN AND BRING ABOUT A MORE PEACEFUL WORLD.
AND IF THEY CAN WIGGLE THAT PHILOSOPHY WITHIN THE VATICAN IT CLEARS THE WAY FOR A POTENTIAL ONE-WORLD ORDER.

Panel 3: ONE OF THE IFSP IDEAS IS TO DEPART FROM THE FEDERAL RESERVE AND ESTABLISH A NEW AND BETTER MONETARY SYSTEM TO HELP ELIMINATE GREED, ENVY AND BETTER SHARING OF INTERNATIONAL RESOURCES.
NOT A BAD IDEA THERE. BUT WHO THEN CONTROLS THE DISTRIBUTED FINANCES.

Panel 4: BUT SOME OF THE WEALTHIER MEMBERS OF VARIOUS COUNTRIES ARE DEFINITELY AGAINST GIVING UP THEIR FINANCIAL INHERITANCE. EVEN THOUGH IT MAY BE WRONG IN THEIR GAINING UNTOLD WEALTH.
FEDERAL RESERVE TYPE PEOPLE?
THEM ... AND OTHERS.

Panel 5: ARE YOU FOR OR AGAINST ALL THIS, PROFESSOR TWIT?
THE REAL QUESTION, ROSCOE, IS ---ARE THESE REALLY ALIENS OR THE FALLEN DEMONS TOSSED OUT OF HEAVEN WORKING TO SET UP WHAT MANY CALL THE ONE-WORLD DISORDER.

Panel 6: NOW I KNOW YOU ARE NOT SAYING THAT ALIENS EXIST, PROFESSOR TWIT. BUT I DO KNOW FOR SURE THAT DEMONS EXIST ... AS 1/3 OF THEM WERE CASTED OUT OF HEAVEN BY THE LORD GOD'S ANGELS AND ARCHANGELS.
YOU GOT THAT RIGHT.

Panel 7: IF ALL THIS DOES COME ABOUT ... THE POPE WILL HAVE TO DECIDE IF THESE ARE BONIFIDE ALIENS OR DEMONS ... IN ORDER TO BAPTIZE THEM IN JESUS' NAME IF THEY SO DESIRE TO HAVE THAT DONE.
GOLLY, PROFESSOR TWIT. THIS COULD BE A REAL JEEPERS CREEPERS SITUATION.

Panel 8: THE VATICAN, BEING A SEPARATE COUNTRY FROM ROME ITSELF, MUST MAKE A DECISION FOR THE WORLD EVEN THOUGH MANY INDEPENDENT RELIGIONS WILL ALSO HAVE THEIR THOUGHTS INTERJECTED INTO WHETHER THESE ARE ALIENS OR DEMONS.
HEY. HOW 'BOUT SPRINKLING HOLY WATER ON THEM TO SEE' IF THEY SKEDADDLE.

Panel 9: A FLEET OF UFO'S FLEW OVER THE WHITEHOUSE FROM JULY 12 TO JULY 29, 1952. THEY WERE SPOTTED BY AN AIRTRAFFIC CONTROLLER AT THE WASHINGTON NAT'L AIRPORT AND ALSO AT THE RONALD REAGAN WASHINGTON NAT'L AIRPORT.
WOW!

Panel 10: DEFINITION OF AN ANGEL IS A SPIRITUAL BEING OF THE LOWEST CELESTRAL ORDER CONSISTING OF SERAPHIMS, CHERUBIMS, THRONES, DOMINIONS VIRTUES, POWERS. PRINCIPALITIES AND OF COURSE THE ANGELS THEMSELVES.
AN ANGEL MAY BE SENT AS A MESSENGER BY GOD AND MAY CONSIST OF WINGS, WHITE ROBES, AND CONVEY BEAUTY, PURITY AND KINDNESS.

Panel 11: DEFINITION OF AN EXTRATERRESTRIAL ALIEN IS DEFINED AS LIFE THAT DID NOT ORIGINATE ON EARTH.
ALSO REFERRED TO AS A SPACE ALIEN THAT RANGES FROM A SIMPLE BACTERIA OR VIRUS --- OR LESS OR FAR MORE COMPLEX THAN AN EARTH HUMAN. CAPABLE OF POTENTIALLY DISAPPEARING FROM EYE VIEW, BUT STILL PRESENT.

Panel 12: DEFINITION OF A DEMON IS AN EVIL SPIRIT A DEVIL (A FALLEN ANGEL) WHO CAN POTENTIALLY POSSESS AND TORMENT A PERSON. DEMONS ARE UNCLEAN BEINGS FROM THE FORCES OF DARKNESS WHICH CAN CAUSE PEOPLE, NATIONS AND EVEN COSMIC DEVESTATION.

OUR MILKY WAY GALAXY IS 100,000 LIGHT YEARS WIDE. ITS THICKNESS AT THE CENTER (WHERE THE BLACK HOLE IS LOCATED) IS 10,000 LIGHT YERS THICK. AND THE TWO ENDS OF THE MILKY WAY ARE 1,000 LIGHT YEARS THICK.

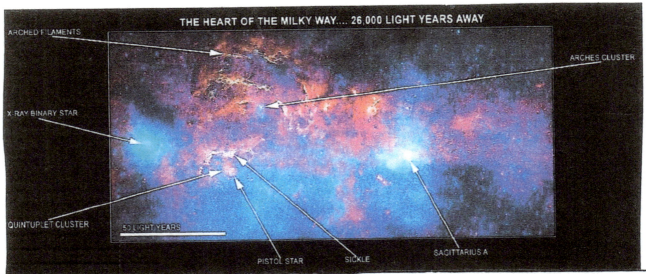

THE HEART OF THE MILKY WAY.... 26,000 LIGHT YEARS AWAY

LET ME GET THIS STRAIGHT PROFESSOR TWIT. SOME SCIENTISTS SAY THAT SPACE ALIENS ARE AROUND 38,000 LIGHT YEARS FROM THE ORION ARM OF THE MILKY WAY ... POSSIBLY IN THE SAGITARIUS ARM AND CAN TRAVEL THERE IN JUST TWO WEEKS.

CORRECT. AND WITH OUR PRESENT MODE OF TRAVEL HERE ON EARTH, IT WOULD TAKE US AROUND 670,000 YEARS TO TRAVE 38,000 LIGHT YEARS.

DO YOU BELIEVE ALL THIS TO BE TRUE.

LET'S LOOK AT THE CHART ONCE AGAIN, ONE HAS TO INCORPORATE SCIENCE, FACT, RELIGION AND FICTION INTO THE EQUATION TO UNCOVER AY SEMBLANCE OF TRUTH.

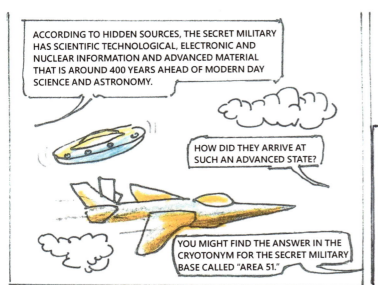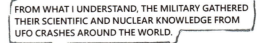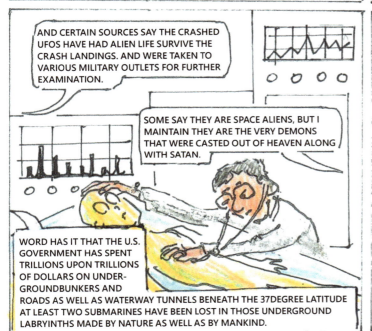

WHAT AN ANGEL LOOKS LIKE.

ANGELS ARE NOT COMPOSED OF PHYSICAL MATTER, BUT ARE SPIRIT BEINGS CREATED BY GOD.

THE ANGEL CAN APPEAR IN HUMAN FORM IF GOD SO PERMITS. IN DANIEL 10:5-6, HE GIVES A PHYSICAL DESCRIPTION OF THE ANGEL HE ACTUALLY SAW.

"I LOOKED UP AND THERE BEFORE ME WAS A MAN DRESSED IN LINEN WITH A BELT OF FINE GOLD FROM UPHAZ AROUND HIS WAIST.

HIS BODY WAS LIKE TOPAZ, HIS FACE LIKE LIGHTNING, HIS EYES LIKE FLAMMING TORCHES HIS ARMS AND LEGS LIKE THE GLEAM OF BURNISHED BRONZE AND HIS VOICE LIKE A MULTITUDE."

HE THEN TOLD ME THAT MICHAEL THE ARCHANGEL HELPED HIM BY FIGHTING AGAINST PRINCE OF EVIL IN ORDER TO REACH ME.

ANGELS ARE NEITHER MALE OR FEMALE. THEY TAKE AN APPEARANCE ALMOST LIKE BOTH PENDING ON WHO SEES THEM.

ALMIGHTY GOD CAN MAKE AN ANGEL SO HORRIBLY FEARFUL THAT EVEN THE DEMONS QUIVER AND SHAKE WHEN THEY SEE THEM.

CHILD SEEING AN ANGEL

ADULT SEEING AN ANGEL

DEMON SEEING AN ANGEL

WHAT A DEMON LOOKS LIKE.

FIRST OF ALL THEY DO NOT HAVE HORNS AND CARRY A PITCHFORK ...ALTHOUGH THE DEVIL CAN DEVISE IT TO BE SO.

YOU CAN MOST GENERALLY UNCOVER A DEMON BY HIS VOLLEY OF ACCUSATIONS ABOUT EVERYONE AND EVERYTHING.

THE NAME 'SATAN' MEANS ACCUSER.

SATAN ACCUSES OTHERS BEFORE GOD DAY AND NIGHT.

SOMETIMES A DEVIL CAN GET BEHIND A PULPIT AND SPEW FALSE DOCTRINE, FOR HE IS THE FATHER OF LIES.

IN EZEKIIEL 28:12-18 GOD FORMERLY DESCRIBED SATAN AS THE SEAL OF PERFECTION; FULL OF WISDOM AND PERFECT IN BEAUTY.

PRECIOUS STONES COVERED HIM SUCH AS GOLD, EMERALDS JASPER AND SO ON.

SATAN, AT ONE TIME, WAS HIGHER THAN MICHAEL AND GABRIEL, BUT HIS PRIDE WAS HIS UNRIGHTEOUS DOWNFALL GATHERING 1/3RD OF THE ANGELS WITH HIM.

DEMONS CAN BE IDENTIFIED BY THEIR IRREVELENT, AND UNGODLY PHILOSOPHY AND LYING TONGUE.

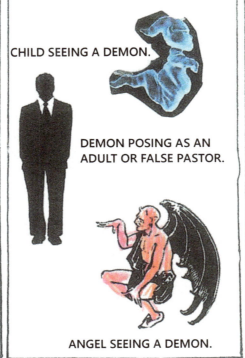

CHILD SEEING A DEMON.

DEMON POSING AS AN ADULT OR FALSE PASTOR.

ANGEL SEEING A DEMON.

WHAT DO SPACE ALIENS LOOK LIKE.

IN GENESIS 1:27 GOD CREATED MANKIND IN HIS OWN IMAGE.

SCI-FI WRITERS AND SCIENTISTS VERY WELL KNOW THAT WE ON EARTH DO NOT HAVE THE TRAVEL TECHNOLOGY TO TRAVEL THOUSANDS OF LIGHT YEARS FROM EARTH.

NOW THERE MAY BE BACTERIA AND VIRUSES ON OTHER PLANETS ... AND THERE MAY BE SPACE ALIENS (OR DEMON) WHO CAN TRAVEL 38,000 LIGHT YEARS IN A MATTER OF ONE WEEK.

AND SOME SCI-FI THINKERS SAY THAT WORMHOLES ALLOW SPACE ALIENS TO TRAVEL LIGHT YEARS DISTANCES BY MERELY USING THEIR MIND AS THE TRAVELLING VEHICLE.

YOU MERELY THINK OF WHERE YOU WANT TO BE AND PRESTO, YOU ARE THERE.

IF ANY SPACE ALIEN HAS VISITED EARTH THEN YOU CAN BE VERY ASSURED THAT THEY ARE FAR, FAR MORE SUPERIOR MENTALLY,

AND THAT THEY CAN TRANSPOSE THEMSELVES INTO PHYSICAL OR SPIRITUAL LIKE BEINGS.

IN OTHERWORDS THEY ARE PRESENT, BUT YOU CANNOT SEE THEM.

THE TEN BASIC DIMENSIONS OF LIFE WILL BE EXPLAINED LATER ABOUT PHYSICAL AND SPIRITUAL TRANSFORMATION.

SPACE ALIENS HAVE BEEN ALLEGEDLY CONVERSING WITH EXO-POLITICAL LEADERS OF EARTH FOR SOME TIME.., BUT ARE DEMONS,

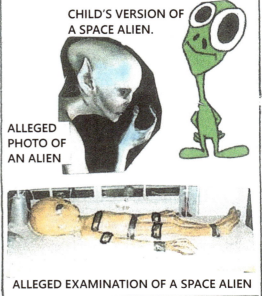

CHILD'S VERSION OF A SPACE ALIEN.

ALLEGED PHOTO OF AN ALIEN

ALLEGED EXAMINATION OF A SPACE ALIEN

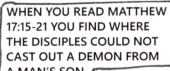

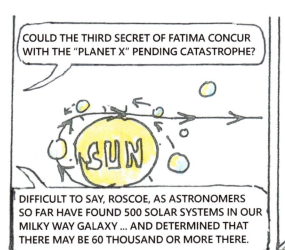
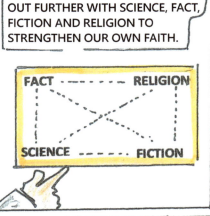

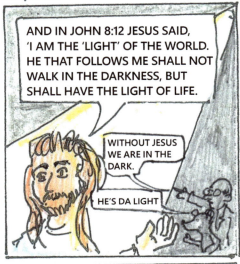

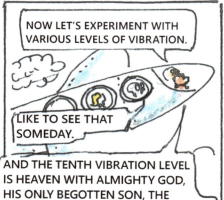

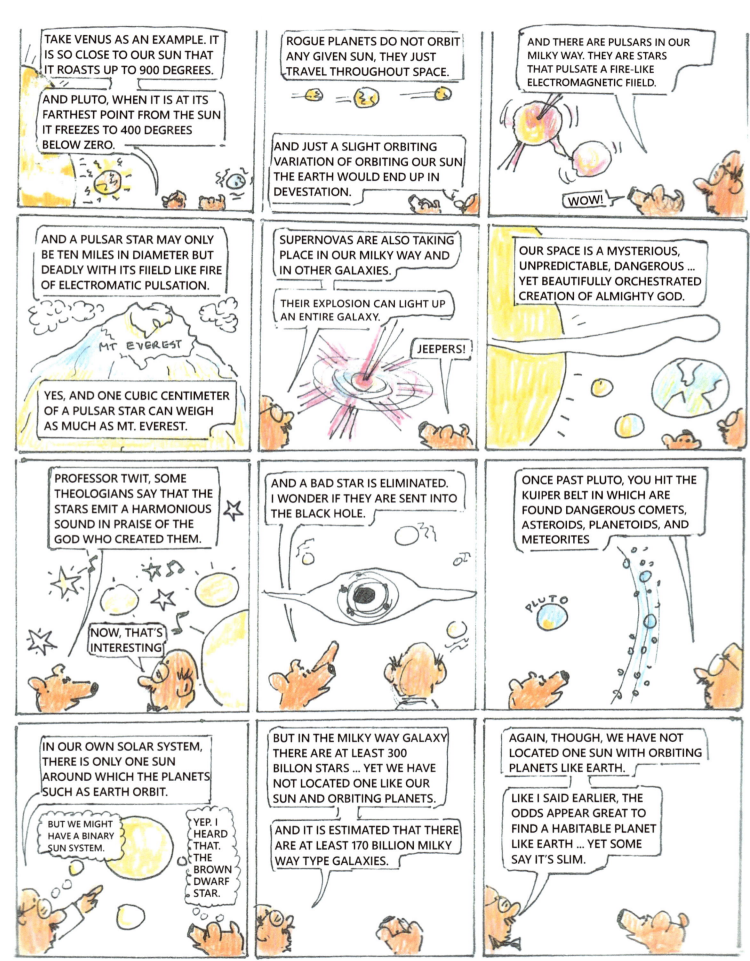

HERE IS AN OUTLINE OF WHAT YOU READ SO FAR.

TOPIC	EXPLANATION	PAGES
(1) **CREATING ROSCOE:**	Professor Twit creates robot Roscoe	1, 2, 3, 4
(2) **TESTING ROSCOE'S IQ:**	Roscoe answers all the questions	4
(3) **BIG BANG VS CREATION:**	God created the Universe and Life	4
(4) **HUBBLE TELESCOPE & VATICAN TELESCOPE:**	comparing the two	4, 5
(5) **TIME THAT THE SUN HITS ALL THE PLANETS:**	Time in minutes	5
(6) **THE ZODIAC:**	Greek name for sculptured animal figures	6
(7) **FACTS ABOUT EARTH, MOON, & SUN:**	Their speed & orbits	6, 7
(8) **INFO ABOUT ZODIAC & MILKY WAY GALAXY:**	Upside down	7
(9) **PLANET X:**	Is it four times the size of Earth & its danger	9, 10
(10) **FACT, FICTION, RELIGION OR SCIENCE:**	you decide for yourself	10
(11) **SIR ISAAC NEWTON STORY:**	Isaac Newton has a toy of Earth	11
(12) **DNA & MILKY WAY INFO:**	God's Omnific Intelligence	12
(13) **CALCULATING THE SPEED OF LIGHT:**	186.000 Miles Per Second	13
(14) **PLANET X ORBIT OF THE SUN:**	God help us if it does	14
(15) **NOAH'S FLOOD AND OTHER PLANET X DESTRUCTION**		15
(16) **SUNS TREMENDOUSLY BIGGER THAN OUR SUN:**	See it yourself	16, 17
(17) **ANGELS TRAVEL 38,000 LIGHT YEARS IN TWO WEEKS**		18
(18) **THE MYSTERIOUS DEMONIC SPIRITS:**	Jesus always wins	20
(19) **PICTURE OF ANGELS, DEMONS, AND ALIENS:**	There are no aliens	21
(20) **VIBRATION LEVELS:**	High vibration levels can make one invisible	23
(21) **THE COMPLETE ARMOR OF GOD:**	Protests His people from Satan	25
(22) **THE BLACK HOLE IN THE GALAXY:**	And Black Matter exists	26

A GOOD REVIEW KEEPS THE FACTS AND FIGURES LIKE BRAND NEW IN YOUR MIND.

AMEN.

YOU CAN SAY THAT AGAIN.

ONE SHOULD GO OVER MATERIAL AT LEAST ONCE OR TWICE A MONTH TO BEST REMEMBER IT.

(27)

Chemtrails

THE LORD JESUS SAID, 'AT THE END TIME THERE WILL BE "SIGNS" AS A FINAL WARNING TIME IS DRAWING NIGH.

THE CHEMTRAIL PLANES FLYING HIGH IN THE SKY ARE SPREADING DEADLY CHEMICALS TO HIDE THE SUN'S TREMENDOUSLY HUGE SOLAR FLARES PERPETRATED BY PLANET X NOW ENTERING INTO OUR SOLAR SYSTEM

RIGHT NOW IT HAS DECIMATED 40% OF THE GLOBAL INSECTS ... AND THAT IS THE VERY FIRST "SIGN" OF THE EVENTUAL MASS DESTRUCTION OF LIFE ON PLANET EARTH.

MOREOVER, THOSE SAME CHEM-TRAIL CHEMICALS ARE EXTREMELY LETHAL TO PEOPLE'S IMMUNE SYSTEM, BRAIN, LUNGS AND OTHER HUMAN FUNCTIONS.

AS YOU ALREADY KNOW, JESUS TOLD THE DISCIPLES, "AT THE END TIME, THE SUN WILL TURN BLACK, THE MOON WILL LOSE ITS LIGHT, AND THE STARS WILL FALL FROM THE SKY.

ZECHARIAH 1:15 ALSO STATED, "THE DAY OF WRATH, A DAY OF TROUBLE AND DISTRESS, DAY OF WASTEFULNESS AND ISOLATION, A DAY OF THICK CLOUDS AND THICK DARKNESS.

SUCH A CATACLYSMIC TIME WAS BROUGHT UPON ATLANTIS, THE SUMERIANS, THE MYANS AS WELL AS SODOM AND GOMORRAH.

ALMIGHTY GOD POURS FORTH SIGNS AS A FINIAL WARNING BEFORE HE CONCLUDES LIFE ON EARTH.

HOWEVER, IF THE GLOBAL PEOPLE REPENT AND ADHERE TO THE PRECEPTS OF GOD, THEN HE WILL BACKSLIDE PLANET X BACK-SLIDE PLANET X OUT OF OUR SOLAR SYSTEM.

Chemtrails

YOU ARE RIGHT DOCTOR NEWT. THOSE WHO REPENT AND ACCEPT JESUS (YESHUA) AS THEIR LORD AND SAVIOR, AND ASK FOR HIS HOLY SPIRIT TO ENTER INTO THEM WILL BE RAPTURE UP BEFORE, IF AND WHEN, PLANET X DESTRUCTIVELY ORBITS OUR SUN.

FOR IT WAS THE HOLY SPIRIT THAT RAISED JESUS FROM THE DEAD, AND THAT SAME HOLY SPIRIT IS HE WHO RAPTURES US UP INTO HEAVEN --- BE WE DEAD OR ALIVE.

AND I WOULD NOT WANT TO BE LEFT ON EARTH ORIN IN THAT GRAVE WHEN THE LORD JESUS RETURNS.

THE WHOLE POINT IS, "DON'T BE SCARED, JUST GET PREPARED," WITH JESUS AS YOUR SAVIOR.

IT IS ALSO IMPERATIVE TO REALIZE THAT ALL THINGS ARE KNOWN BY ALMIGHTY GOD BEFORE, DURING AND AFTER ALL SITUATIONS. IN FACT, THE LORD GOD CREATES SITUATIONS AND ALSO SOLVES THEM.

SO IT IS WISE TO BE IN TUNE WITH HIS WORD TO THWART AND BE FAR AND AWAY FROM SATAN, THE BEAST, THE ANTICHRIST AND HIS DEMONS.

AND LET'S NOT DISCOUNT ALL THE VOLCANOES, HURRICANES, TSUNAMIS, FLOODS AND TORNADOES AS EVIDENCES OF GOD'S 'SIGNS.

WOE, WOE, UNTO THOSE WHO SEE NOT THE "SIGNS" AND DO NOT REPENT.

SHOWN HERE ARE SOME OF THE VARIOUS KINDS OF STARS
IN OUR UNIVERSE --- OTHER THAN OUR SUN.

1. Main Sequence Stars

A SEQUENCE STAR IS ONE LIKE OUR SUN WHICH DERIVED ITS BEGINNING ONCE NUCLEAR FUSION STARTS IN ITS CORE, OUR SUN HAS BEEN IN SEQUENCE FOR 5 BILLION YEARS.

2. Red Giant Stars

A RED STAR IS ONE THAT HAS USED UP ALL ITS HYDROGEN FUEL AND BECOMES A RED GIANT. AS IT OSCILLATES, THE STAR CAN BECOME A WHITE DRAWF OR AN EVENTUAL BLACK HOLE.

3. White Dwarfs

A WHITE DWARF STAR IS ONE THAT WAS A RED GIANT BUT OVER TIME AS THAT STAR EMERGES INTO SPACE EVENTUALLY ALL THAT BECOMES LEFT TO THE STAR IS ITS CORE.

4. Neutron Stars

A NEUTRON STAR IS A MASSIVE STAR THAT LOST NUCLEAR FUEL AND BECOMES LIKE A SUPERNOVA LEAVING BEHIND A VERY DENSE CORE WHERE IT IS SIMILAR TO A BLACK HOLE BUT NOT AS DENSE.

5. Black Holes

A BLACK HOLE ARE MASSIVE STARS COLLAPSING IN ON THEMSELVES DUE TO THE GRAVITY OF A GIANT SUPERNOVA THAT SUCKS IN THE CLOSE BY ORBITING STARS.

6. Brown Dwarfs

BROWN DWARF STARS ARE STARS THAT NEVER ACCUMULAATE ENOUGH MASS TO IGNITE NUCLEAR FUSION IN THEIR CORE.

7. Variable Stars

VARIABLE STARS MAINTAIN A CONSTANT BRIGHTNESS DUE TO ATMOSPHERIC EFFECTS AS WELL AS THEIR ROTATION.

A SUPERNOVA STAR IS ONE THT BURSTS AND EXPLODES WHEN IT CAN NO LONGER HANDLE ITS NUCLEAR FUEL.
THE EXPLOSION EMITS A LIGHT BRIGHTER THAN THAT OF A GALAXY AND ALSO EMITS MORE RADIATING ENERGY THAN OUR SUN.
THE EXPLOSION OF A SUPERNOVA STAR PROVIDES THE HEAVY ELEMENTS OF THE UNIVERSE.

A PULSAR STAR IS HIGHLY MAGNETIZED AND ITS ROTATING MOVEMENT EMITS A ELECTROMAGNETIC FIELD OF RADIATION. PULSAR STARS ARE VERY DENSE IN WEIGHT. JUST A SPOONFUL CAN WEIGH AS MUCH AS Mt. EVEREST, AND IT RIVALS AN ATOMIC CLOCK IN KEEPING PERFECT TIME.

IN PSALM 147:4, THE LORD GOD DETERMINES THE NUMBER OF STARS, AND HE GIVES TO EACH THEIR NAME.

INTIMATELY ALL ENERGY, POWER AND LIFE ???ME INTO THE PHYSICAL WORLD, BUT ITS ???URCE STEMS FROM THE SPIRITUAL WORLD.

ALMIGHTY GOD PROVIDES REVELATIONS TO MANKIND SO HIS PEOPLE DO NOT PERISH BUT MANY ASPECTS OF HEAVEN ARE OUT OF BOUNDS FOR MANKIND TO EVEN UNDERSTAND.

AS FOR ME, I AM STILL WONDERING HOW SATAN TRAVELLED FROM THE EARTH TO HEAVEN TO SPEAK WITH GOD.

[Solar system diagram with labels: PLUTO, NEPTUNE, URANUS, SATURN, JUPITER, MARS, EARTH, VENUS, MERCURY, SUN]

PLANET X (NIBIRU) — ALLEGEDLY NASA HAS BEEN AWARE OF PLANET X FOR THE PAST 30 YEARS

BROWN DWARF STAR

FUN SUN FACTS

The sun is spinning on its axis 4,400 MPH and is orbiting the inner core of the Milky Way Galaxy at a speed of 480,000 MPH.

- THE SUN ACCOUNTS FOR 99.8% OF THE MASS OF OUR SOLAR SYSTEM.
- THE SUN IS 74% HYDROGEN 24 HELIUM, AND THE REST INCLUDES TRACES OF IRON, NICKKEL, OXYGEN. ETC.
- THE SUN IS CONTINUOUSLY HEATING UP 10% MORE LUMINOUS EVERY BILLION YEARS.
- A LAUNCHED SPACECRAFT IN 1995 CALLED THE SOLAR & HILIOSCOPE OBERVATORY (BUILT BY NASA AND ESA) OBSERVES THE SUN.
- ONE MILLION EARTHS CAN FIT INSIDE THE SUN.
- LIGHT FROM THE SUN TAKES 8 MINUTES AND 20 SECONDS TO HIT THE EARTH.
- THE SUN IS ABOUT 25,000 LIGHT YEARS FROM THE GALACTIC CENTER AND IT TAKES THE SUN 250 MILLION YEARS TRAVELLING AT A SPEED AROUND 500,000 MPH TO COMPLETELY ORBIT THE INNER CORE OF THE MILKY WAY GALAXY.

- ALL ENERGY COMES FROM THE SUN.
- THE SUN IS ONLY ONE OF 200 BILLION STARS IN OUR MILKY WAY GALAXY. SOME SAY 500 BILLION STARS.
- ALL THE PLANETS IN OUR SOLAR SYSTEM ORBIT AROUND THE SUN.
- THE SUN SPINS ON ITS AXIS 4,040 MPH.
- THE SUN TRAVELS THROUGH THE MILKY WAY AT A SPEED OF 500,000 MPH.
- THE LARGEST STAR IN OUR GALAXY IS THE CANIS MAJORIS WHICH IS 1,500 TIMES LARGER THAN OUR SUN.
- ONY 55% OF THE AMERICANS KNOW THAT THE SUN IS A STAR.

- OUR SUN IS A COMMON, MIDDLE-SIZED STAR.
- ALL THE PLANETS IN OUR SOLAR SYSTEM ORBIT THE SUN COUNTERCLOCKWISE AND ROTATE CLOCKWISE. VENUS, HOWEVER, ORBITS THE SUN CLOCKWISE
- THERE ARE LIKELY ABOUT 60,000+ TYPE SOLAR SYSTEMS LIKE OURS IN THE MILKY WAY GALAXY
- EVERY SO OFTEN A PATCH OF PARTICLES WILL BURST FROM THE SUN AND CAN DISRUPT SATELLITE COMMUNICATIONS AND EVEN KNOCK OUT POWER ON THE EARTH.
- THE SUN ROTATES ON ITS AXIS EVERY 25.38 EARTH DAYS.
- HUMAN LIFE GETS ITS ENERGY AND LIFE FROM THE "SUN", WATER AND FOOD. BUT WITHOUT THE SON OF GOD THERE WOULD BE NO SUN … AS HE CREATED IT ALONG WITH MANKIND.

- NO SOLAR ECLIPSE CAN LAST LONGER THAN 7 MINUTES, 58 SECONDS BECAUSE OF THE SPEED IN WHICH THE SUN TRAVELS.
- THE AZTECS BELIEVED THE SUN DIED EACH AND EVERY NIGHT AND NEEDED HUMAN BLOOD TO GIVE IT STRENGTH TO RISE THE NEXT DAY. SO THEY SACRIFICED 15,000 MEN A YEAR TO APPEASE THEIR SUN GOD.
- THE SUN PROVIDES AROUND 126,000,000,000,000 HORSE POWER OF ENERGY EVERY DAY.
- THE SUN LIGHT IS WHITE BUT APPEARS YELLOW FROM THE BLUE HUES OF THE EARTH.
- THE SUN ROTATES COUNTERCLOCK WISE,
- THE DIAMETRER OF OUR SUN IS 864,308 MILES WIDE WITH A CIRCUMFERENCE OF 2,713,406 MILES. THE DIAMETER OF THE VT CANIS MAJORITY SUN IS 1,815,087,390 MILES WIDE AND IT IS 5,000 LIGHT YEARS FROM OUR SUN. LITERALLY MILIIONS OF OUR SUN CAN BE PUT INSIDE SOME OF MAMMOYH STARS (SUNS) IN THE UNIVERSE.

(31)

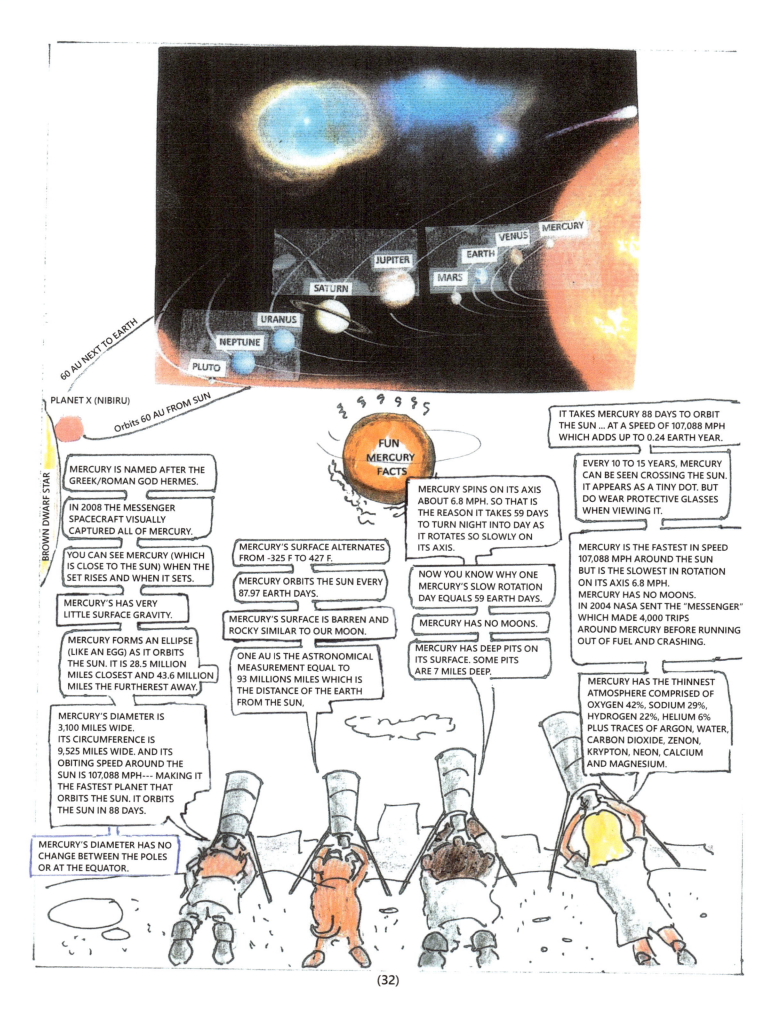

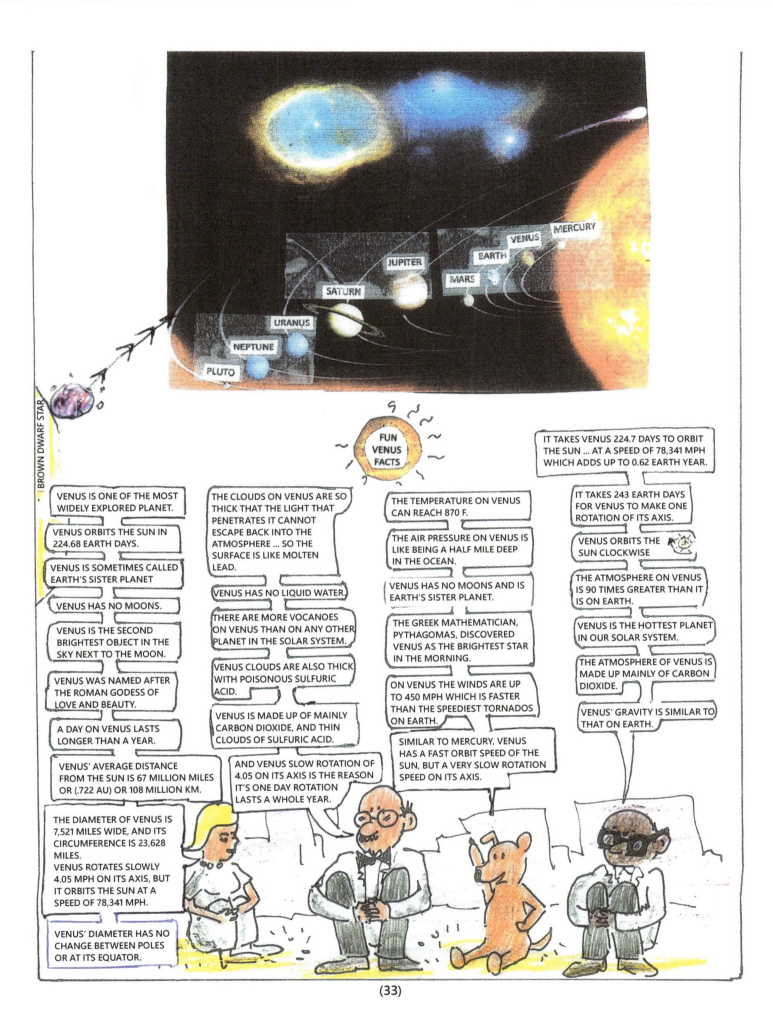

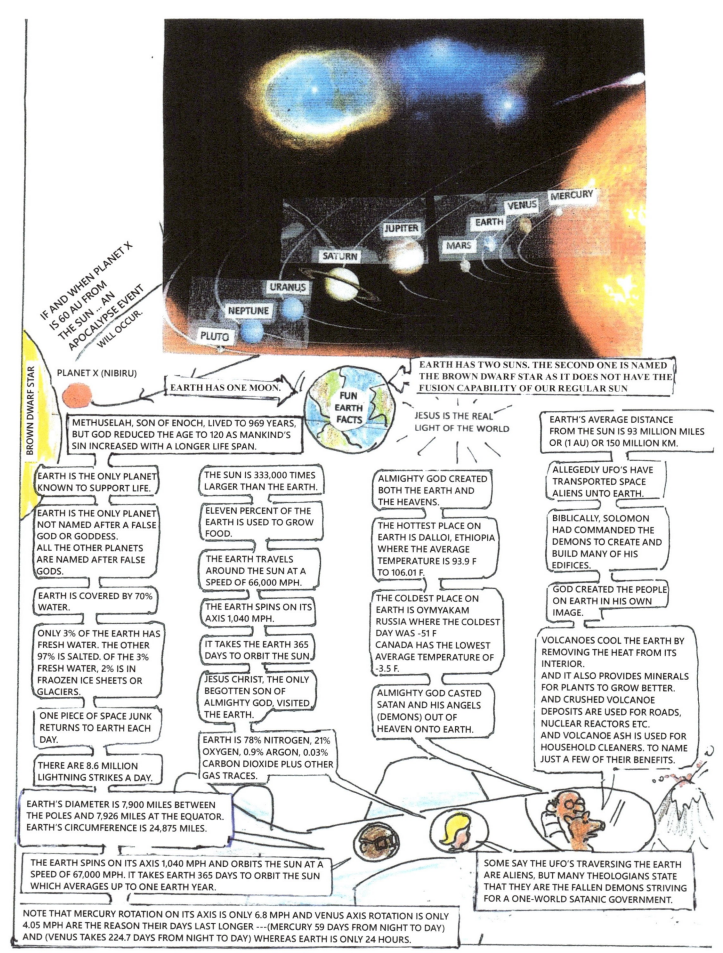

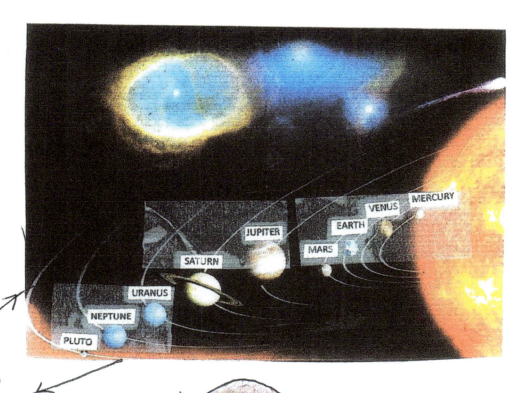

PLANE X ORBITS NEAR THE SUN EVERY 2,160 YEARS

PLANET X (NIBIRU)

BROWN DWARF STAR

MARS HAS TWO MOONS

FUN MARS FACTS

IT TAKES MARS 687 DAYS TO ORBIT THE SUN ... AT A SPEED OF 58,000 MPH WHICH ADDS UP TO 1.88 EARTH YEARS.

MAR'S AVERAGE DISTANCE FROM THE SUN IS 143 MILLION MILES OR (1.52 AU) OR 228 MILLION KM.

AS OF 2014, NO HUMAN BEING HAS SET FOOT ON MARS.

IT TAKES MARS 686.98 EARTH DAYS TO ORBIT THE SUN.

THE CANYON ON MARS IS CALLED VALLEY MARINIUS IS 2,500 MILES LONG AND 4.5 MILES DEEP.
THE GRAND CANYON IS 500 MILES LONG AND ONE MILE DEEP.

MARS HAS TWO MOONS NAMED PHOBOS AND DEIMOS.

IT TAKES ABOUT 16 MONTHS TO TRAVEL TO AND FROM MARS. EIGHT MONTHS TO AND EIGHT MONTHS TO RETURN.

MARS ROTATES ON ITS AXIS EVERY 24.6 DAYS.

THE DIAMETER OF MARS IS 4,222 MILES WIDE.

MARS IS MORE SIMILAR TO EARTH THAN ANY OTHER PLANET IN OUR SOLAR SYSTEM.

SCIENTISTS ARE LOOKING AT MARS AS A PLACE WHERE EVENTUAL HUMAN LIFE MAY EXIST SINCE OUR POPULATION IS EXPONENTIATING

PRESENTLY. MARKS IS THE MOST EXPLORED PLANET. YET MANKIND HAS YET TO STEP FOOT ON IT.

IN 2012, THE SPACECRAFT CURIOSITY ROVER LANDED ON MARS TO DETERMINE WHETHER IT HAD ANY MICROBIAL LIFE.

THE ATMOSPHERE ON MARS IS 95% CARBON DIOXIDE.

MARS HAS A 24 HOUR DAY BUT ITS YEAR IS 687 DAYS LONG.

HOWEVER, OTHER RESEARCH TEAMS SAY THAT THE ENTIRE POPULATION OF THE UNITED STATES COLD FIT QUITE EASILY INSIDE THE STATE OF TEXAS.

THE MOUNTAIN ON MARS CALLED OLYMPUS MONS (AN EXTINCT VOCANO) REACHES UPWARDS TO 17 MILES HIGH. IT IS 3 TIMES THE HEIGHT OF MT. EVEREST.

MARS HAS A RED COLOR (CAUSED BY IRON OXIDE) SO IT WAS NAMED AFTER THE ROMAN GOD OF BLOOD AND WAR, ARES.

MARS IS CARBON DIOXIDE 95%, NITROGEN 2.7%, ARGON 1.6%, OXYGEN 0.13 % WATER 0.01%

NASA IS PRESENTLY PLANNING AN EVENTUAL SPACECRAFT TO LAND MAN ON MARS.

I HAVE TO THINK SERIOUSLY ABOUT THE WORDS OF ROSCOE, WHEN HE SPOKE ABOUT PSALMS 8:3 WHERE GOD SAID, "WHEN YOU LOOK AT THE SKY WHICH I HAVE CREATED, YOU SEE THE MOON AND STARS WHICH I HAVE SET IN PLACE."
YES, INDEED, ROSCOE, GOD'S GREATNESS IS SEEN IN ALL THE WORLD.

THE CIRCUMFERENCE OF MARS IS 13,263 MILES. IT ROTATES ON ITS AXIS AT A SPEED OF 539.4 MPH

MAR'S DIAMETER IS 4,196.3 MILES BETWEEN THE POLES AND 4,220.6 MILES AT THE EQUATOR.

DID I REALLY HEAR PROFESSOR TWIT, PROFESS GOD'S CREATION OF THE UNIVERSE.
MY, OH MY. WILL WONDERS EVER CEASE. PRAISE GOD?

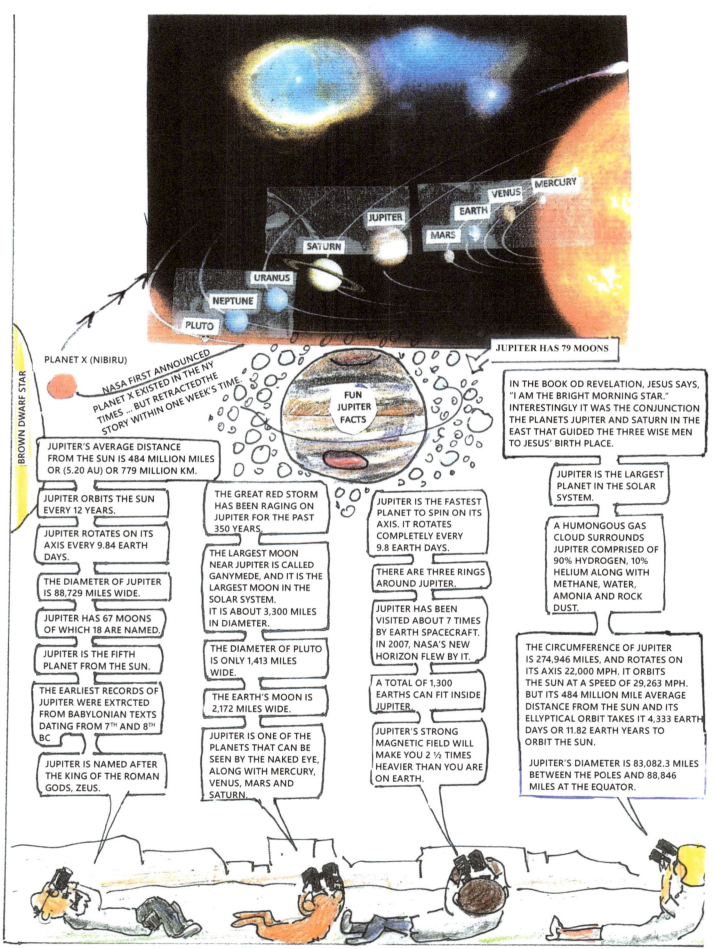

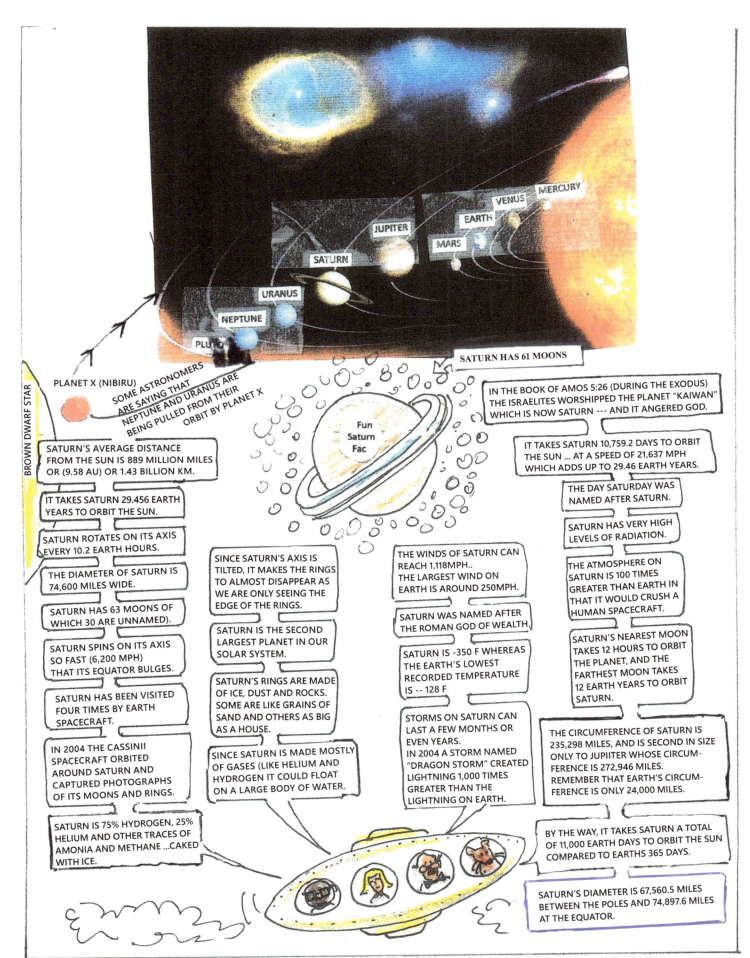

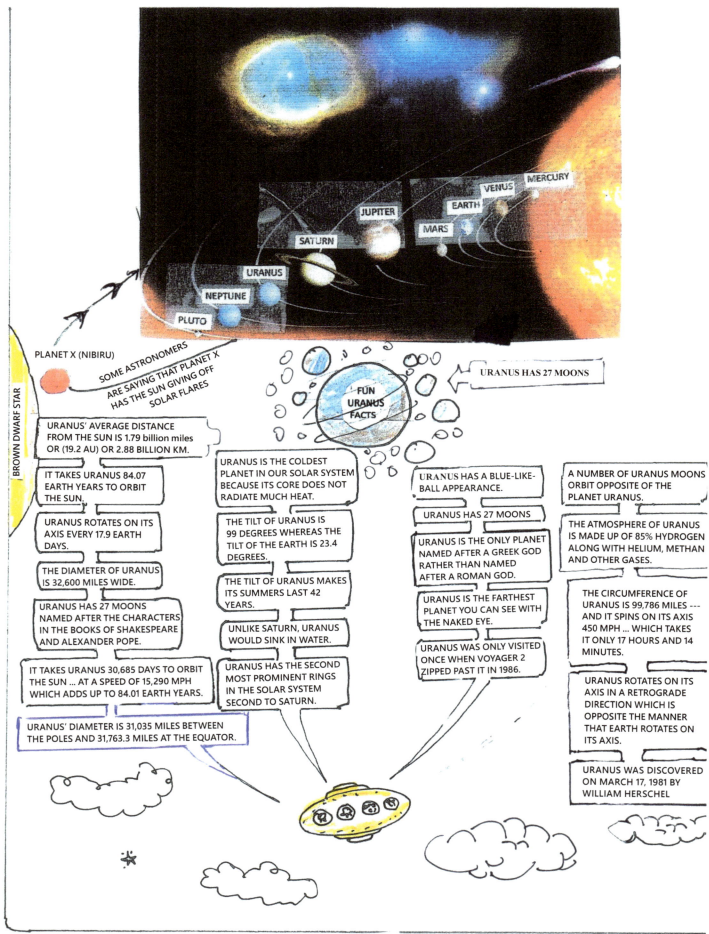

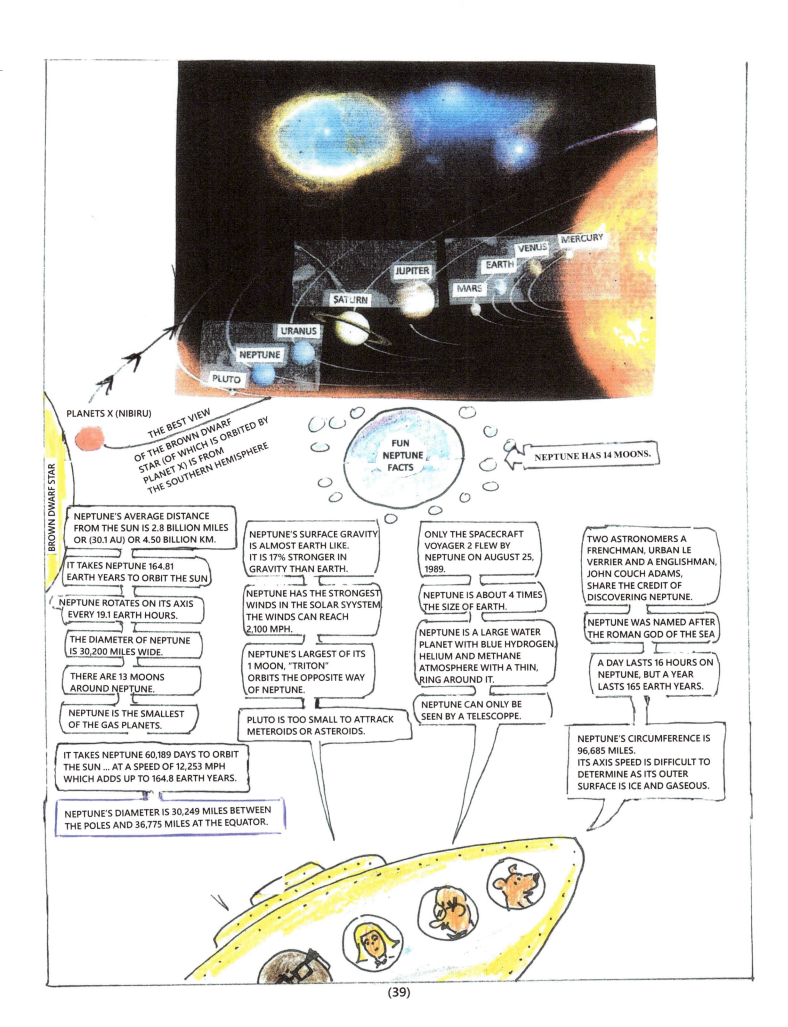

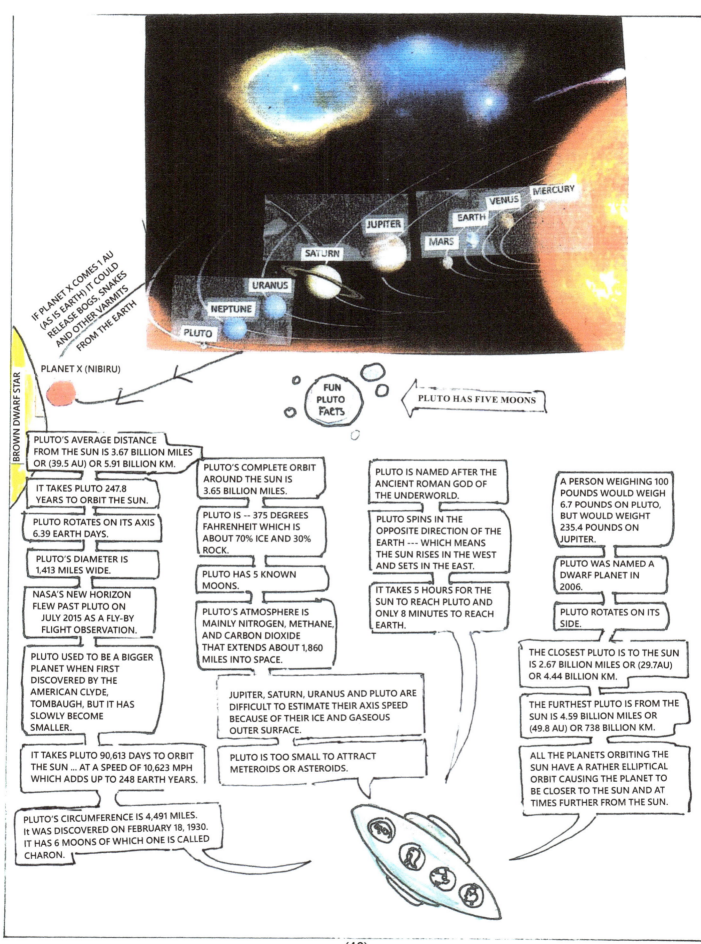

SPANISH ASTRONOMERS CLAIM O HAVE FOUND THE BROWN DWARD STAR, BUT HAVE NOT SUBMITTED WRITTEN EVIDENCE.
NASA RETRACTED THAT IT FOUND THE BROWN DWARF STAR IN 1982.

THE BROWN DWARF STAR IS VISIBLE EVERY 2,160 YEARS.

PLANET X (NIBIRU)

Solar system diagram labeled: SUN, MERCURY, VENUS, EARTH, MARS, JUPITER, SATURN, URANUS, NEPTUNE, PLUTO.

FUN MOON FACTS

- THE MOON IS OF GREAT VALUE TO THE EARTH IN TERMS OF AFFECTING THE TIDES OF OCEANS AND WATERWAYS. IT HAS PLATINUM AND GOLD WORTH $1,000 AN OUNCE, AND IT HAS A HUGE SUPPLY OF HELIUM -3 WHICH IS A MAJOR FUEL FOR NUCLEAR FUSION --- AS WELL AS MANY OTHER VALUABLE ASSETS.
- THERE ARE NO VOLCANOES ON THE MOON.
- THERE ARE HUNDREDS OF MOONQUAKES ON THE MOON.
- SCIENTISTS BELIEVE THAT THE CENTER OF THE MOON IS JUST A BIG CAVITY
- WHENEVER THE UNMANNED APOLLO 11 CRASHED LANDED ON THE MOON, THE MOON VIBRATED FOR THREE HOURS.
- THE MOON HAS NO ATMOSPHERE SO IT IS UNPROTECTED FROM COSMIC RAYS, ASTEROIDS, AND SOLAR WINDS.
- THE MOON IS ABOUT 240,250 MILES FROM THE EARTH.
- THE MOON ORBITS THE EARTH EVERY 27.3 EARTH DAYS.
- A 100 LB. PERSON WOULD WEIGHT 16.5 LBS ON THE MOON.
- THE SAME SIDE OF THE MOON ALWAYS FACES THE EARTH.
- THE MOON HAS A DIAMETER OF 2,172 MILES WIDE.
- TWELVE MEN HAVE WALKED ON THE MOON. NEIL ARMSTRONG (ON APOLLO 11) WAS THE FIRST.
- THE MOON (2,160 MILES WIDE) IS SMALLER THAN JUPITER'S MOON (3,400 MILES WIDE) AND SATURN'S MOON TITAN (ABOUT 3,100 MILES WIDE)
- IN 2019, NASA IS WORKING ON PUTTING A SPACE STATION ON THE MOON.

BROWN DWARF STAR

- THE MOON ORBITS THE EARTH EVERY 27.6 HOURS AT A SPEED OF 2,288 MPH OR 3,673 KM.
- THE MOON ORBITS THE SUN (LIKE THE EARTH) EVERY 356.26 DAYS AT A SPEED OF 67,000 MPH
- THE AVERAGE DISTANCE OF THE MOON FROM THE SUN IS 93MILLION MILES.

- WITHOUT THE MOON, THE EARTH COULD PERISH.
- THERE ARE (WHAT APPEARS TO BE) MAN-MADE OR SPACE ALIEN TYPE SHARDS AND HIGH CONSTRUCTED OBELISKS ON THE MOON.
- THE MOON IS ABOUT 93 MILLION MILES FROM THE SUN.

PLANETS	NUMBER OF MOONS
MERCURY	0
VENUS	0
EARTH	1
MARS	2
JUPITER	63
SATURN	62
URANUS	27
NEPTUNE	13
PLUTO	2

HYPOTHETICALLY THERE IS A BROWN DWARF STAR ABOUT 20% THE SIZE OF OUR SUN WHICH HAS 7 PLANETS ORBITING IT. IT IS LOCATED ABOUT 4 TO 6 TIMES AS FAR AWAY AS THE PLUTO, BUT IS STILL WITHIN THE GRAVITATIONAL PULL OF THE SUN. THE BD STAR IS NEAR OR BEYOND THE OORT CLOUD. THE BROWN DWARF STAR COMES WITHIN 60 AU OF EARTH, THEN ONE OF ITS SEVEN PLANETS CALLED PLANET X OR NIBIRU TRAVELS ANOTHER 60 AU RIGHT IN LINE WITH THE ORBIT OF PLANET EARTH --- CAUSING GREAT DESTRUCTION. SOME ASTRONOMERS SAY THE BROWN DWARF STAR ORBITS NEAR EARTH EVERY 2,160 YEARS ... AND THE SECOND BROWN DWARF STAR ORBIT OF 2,160 YEARS IS WHEN MASS DEVASTATION TAKES PLACE ON EARTH.
HOWEVER, SOME SCIDNTISTS MAINTAIN THE BROWN DWARF STAR ORBITS COMPLETELY AROUND THE SUN EVERY 3,600 YEARS (NOT JUST 60 AU AWAY FROM THE EARTH)
IN EITHER CASE AND IF EITHER IS RIGHT, A GIGANTIC APOCALYPSE WILL TAKE PLACE ON EARTH.
MANY THEOLOGIANS SAY THAT GOD'S HOLY SPIRIT WILL RAPTURE UP ALL THE 'BORN AGAIN' BELIEVERS IN JESUS CHRIST BEFORE THE COLLIDING OF THE PLANETS.

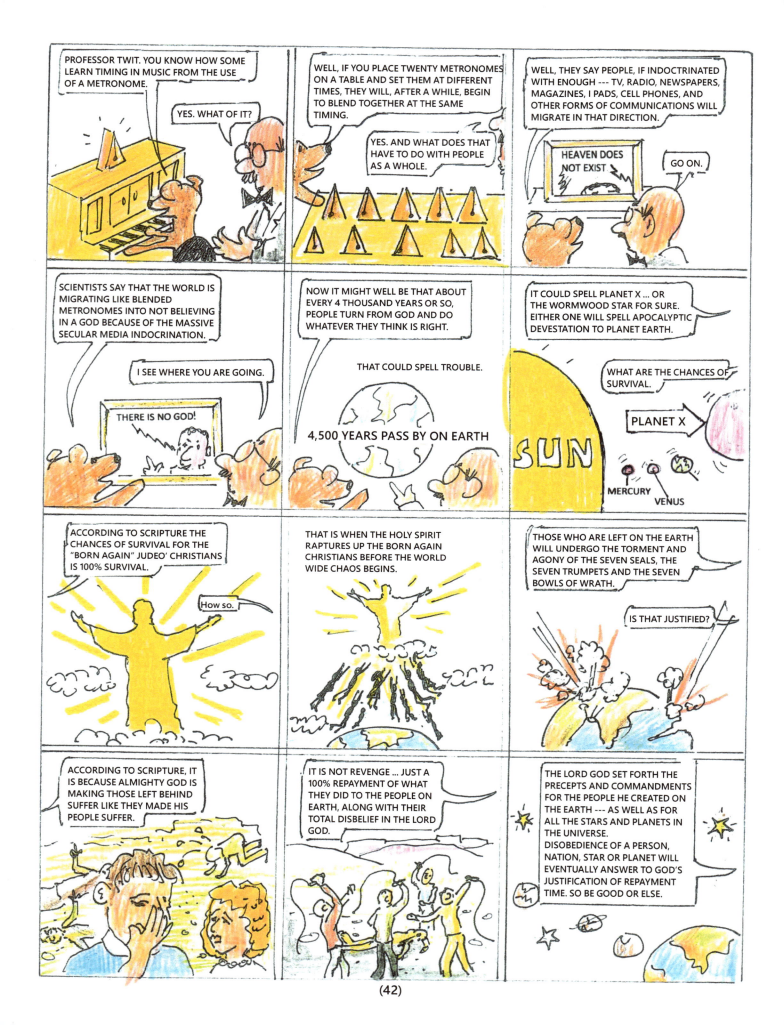

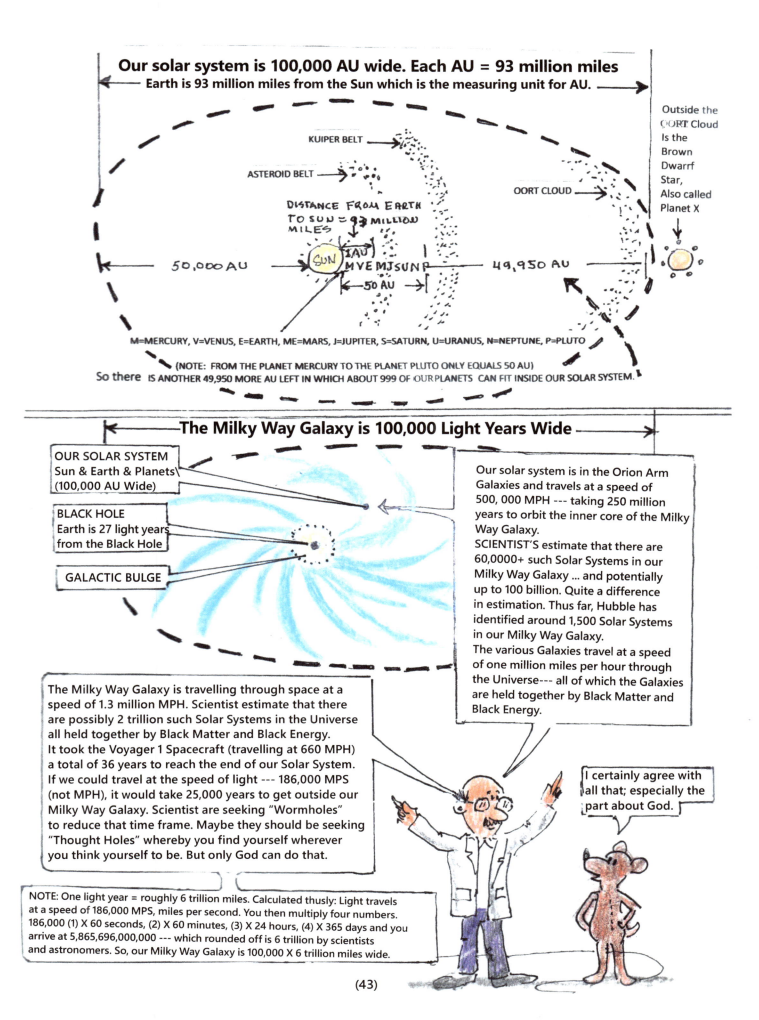

(44)

HERE IS AN OUTLINE OF WHAT YOU READ SO FAR.

TOPIC   EXPLANATION   PAGES

(1) **CHEMTRAILS:** Toxic chemicals sprayed across the globe that cause forest fires to explode, and infects people with heart, chest and other sickness 28

(2) **THE VARIOUS KINDS OF STARS IN THE UNIVERSE** Amazing Stars 29

(3) **MILKY WAY GALAXY:** Milky Way Galaxy is 100,000 light years wide, and our Solar System is presently in the Orion Arm of the Milky Way Galaxy. Our Milky Galaxy travels One million miles per hour through the Universe 30

(4) **SUN FACTS:** the Sun is 864,308 miles wide, and spins on it axis 4,400 MPH and orbits the inside of the Milky Way Galaxy at a speed of 483,000 MPH and takes about 250,000 years to orbit the inside of our Milky Way Galaxy 31

(5) **MERCURY FACTS:** Spins on ts axis 6.8 MPH, and is 9,525 miles wide. It takes 88 days at a speed of 107,088 MPH to orbit the Sun. It is the fastest planet to orbit the Sun. Mercury is 28.5 to 43.6 million miles from the sun (Pending its orbiting path) 32

(6) **VENUS:** Spins on its axis every 4.05 MPH, and is 5,7521 miles wide. It takes it 224.68 days at a speed of 78,341 MPH to orbit the Sun. Venus is 67 million from the Sun 33

(7) **EARTH:** Spins on its axis 1.040 MPH, and is 7,900 miles wide. It takes 365 days to orbit the Sun. Earth is (ideally) 93 million miles from the sun. Earth is the only planet known to support human life. Earth rotation is 24 hours from night to day; Mercury's slow 6.8 MPH rotation takes 59 days from night to day, while Venus; slow rotation of 4.05 MPH takes 224.7 days from night to day ... 34

(8) **MARS:** Spins on its axis 539.4 MPH, and is 4,222 miles wide. It takes 686.98 days at a speed of 539.4 MPH to orbit the Sun. Mars is 143 million miles from the Sun. Mars diameter id smaller than Mercury as well as Venus 35

(9) **JUPITER:** Spins on its axis every 9.84 Earth Days, and is 88,729 miles wide. It orbits the Sun every 12 years. At a speed of 29,263 MPH. Jupiter is about 484 million miles from the Sun. You can see Jupiter with your naked eye as well as Mercury, Venus, Mars and Uranus. Jupiter is the largest planet in our Solar System. There are three rings around Jupiter 36

(10) **SATURN:** Spins on its axis 6,200 MPH, and is 74,600 miles wide. It takes 10,759.2 days to orbit the Sun at a speed of 21,637 MPH. Saturn is 889 million miles from the Sun. Saturn has 63 moons. Saturn axis and rings are tilted 37

(11) **URANUS:** Spiin ns on its axis every 17.9 Earth days, and is 31,763.3 miles wide. It orbits the Sun 30,685 days at a speed of 15,290 MPH. It is 1;7 billion miles from the Sun. Uranus axis is also tioted 38

(12) **NEPTUNE:** Spins on its axis every 19.1 Earth hours, and is 30,200 miles wide. It takes Neptune 60,180 days s to orbit the Sun as a speed of 12,253 MPH. Neptune is 2.8 billion miles from the Sun. Neptune has the strongest winds of 2,100 MPH 39

HERE IS AN OUTLINE OF WHAT YOU READ SO FAR.

TOPIC   **EXPLANATION**   **PAGES**

(13) **PLUTO:** Spins on its axis every 6.39 days, and it is 1,413 miles wide. It takes 90,613 days to orbit the Sun at a speed of 10,623 MPH. Pluto is 3.67 billion or 4.59 billion miles from the Sun. Pluto is -375 degrees Fahrenheit which make it 70% ice and 30% rock. A person weighing 100mpounds will weight 6.7 pounds on Pluto but weight 235,4 pounds on Jupiter. NOTE: It takes the Sun 5 hours to reach Pluto and only 8 minutes to reach Earth **40**

(14) **MOON:** Spins on its axis every 27 days, and is 2.172 miles wide. The moon orbits the Earth every 27.6 hours at a speed of 2,288 MPH. The moon orbits the Sun (like the Earth) every 365.26 days at a speed of 67,000h. MPH. The Moon affects the tides of the Ocean, and has Platinum and God worth $1,000 per ounce. The Moon is about 240,250 miles from Earteh **41**

(15) **THE METRONOME MESMERIZES AS DONE TV HYPNOTIZES PEOPLE, BUT THOSE "BORN AGAIN" ARE SAVED.** A set of Metronomes can blend into one sound as does TV, News Papers, Cell Phones, Computers, Radio, Magazines, etc can make people hypnotically migrate away common sense regarding politics, country and the will of God. But those who are "Born Again" will be saved **42**

(16) **SOLAR SYSTEM, MILKY WAY GALAXY FACTS:** Our Solar System is 100,000 AU Wide. AN AU equals 93 million miles. Tht is the distance of Planet Earth to the Sun. The Sun is in the middle of our Solar System with 50 million on one side and 50 million AU on the side where our nine planets are located. Earth is 93 Million miles from the Sun and Pluto is 3.67 billion to 4.50 billion miles from the Sun. The Sun's rays hit Pluto in 5 hours whereas the Sun hits Earth in 8 minutes. There are approximately 49,950 more AU yet to be discovered in our Solar System. And Planet X (also Called the Brown Dwarf Star (BDS); It lies outside our Solar System, but is now dangerously traveling inside our Solar System right now, If the BDS eventually orbits our Sun it will upset the Teutonic Planets and the volcanoes will go off and blacken he Sun, make the Moon lose its light, and the asteroids between Mars and Jupiter will catastrophically plummet the Earth, Our Milky Way Galaxy is 100,000 light years wide. Every Light Year equals approximately 6 trillion miles. It takes our Solar System 250 million years to orbit the inside of our Milky Way Galaxy. Our Solar System is right now in the Orion Arm of the Milky Wy Galaxy. Planet X (the BDS) enters our Solar System every 2,300 to 3,000+ yers whenever humankind exe=exceeds the unrighteousness of Sodom & Gomorrah **43**

(17) **PLANET X WILL POLARIZE OUR ENTIRE EARTH:** If Planet X orbits our Sun, it will set off the thousands of volcanoes that will blacken the Sun, make the Moon lose its light, and the asteroids between Mars and Jupiter will plummet the Earth, The Ocean will expand and divide the earth into two separate sections **44**

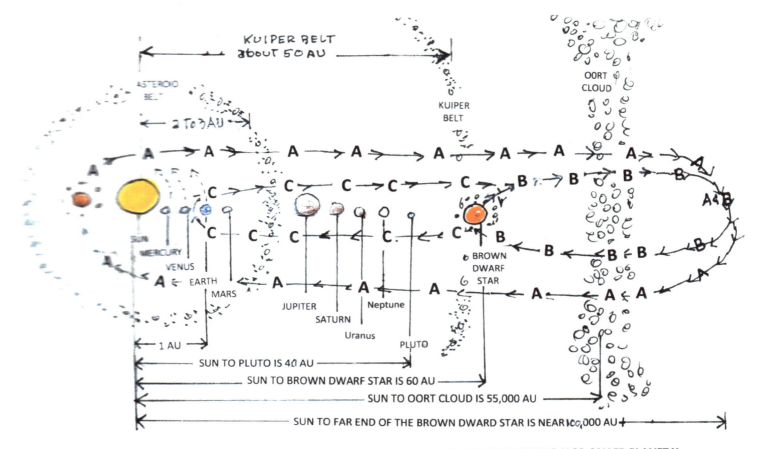

THE BROWN DWARF STAR IS ALSO CALLED PLANET X

The above illustration shows the orbits of A, B & C. Orbit "B" is the orbit of the Brown Dwarf Star, BDS. In this illustration, the Brown Dwarf Star is around 95,000 AU from the Sun.

The magnetic force of the Sun, pulls the Brown Dwarf Star within 60 Au of it.

Then one of the seven planets that orbits the BDS, called Nemesis, (which is the orbit of "C") breaks away and travels another 60 Au right smack dab in the same orbit of Earth.

Now, both Earth and the break-away-planet Nemesis are 1 AU from the Sun. Both planets are now 93 million miles from the Sun and are on a collusion course --- as the Earth travels counterclockwise of the Sun ... and Planet Nemesis travels clockwise to the sun. Such a diversified orbiting can cause a catastrophic collision.

According to some astronomers the magnetic pull of the Sun on The Brown Dwarf Star (along with its breakaway planet Nemesis) generally occurs every 2,160 YEARS.

THIS BRINGS UP --- DO WE LIVE WITH A POTENTIALLY DANGEROUS BINARY SUN IN OUR SOLAR SYSTEM? SOME ASTRONOMERS BELIEVE SO, AS SPACE EXPLOTATION VEHICLES LIKE HUBBLE ARE DOCUMENTING THAT ABOUT HALF OF THE SOLAR SYSTEM SYSTEMS IN OUR MILKY WAY GALAXY HAVE TWO SUNS. MOST GENERALLY THE SECOND SUN IS A BROWN DWARF TYPE STAR THAT DOES NOT HAVE THE FUSION CAPABJILITIES OF THE MAIN SUN.

THE BROWN DWARF STAR IS ALSO CALLED PLANET X

However, some astronomers think differently. They conclude that the Brown Dwarf Star is illustrated by the "A" orbit only.

Again, the Brown Dwarf Star, BDS, is around 95,000 AU from the Sun. The Sun's magnetic strength pulls the BDS (and its seven orbiting planets) completely around the Sun.

Remember that the BDS is travelling clockwise while orbiting the Sun (whereas most of the regular planets such as Mercury, Earth, Mars Jupiter, etc. are orbiting the Sun counter clockwise, but Venus orbits clock wise.

According to calculations (if the BDS does completely orbit the Sun) this will occur every 2,160 years.

The result will bring about an even bigger catastrophic collusion.

Many theologians (and scientists) conclude that Earth will eventually have a dooms day. (Not if ... but when!)

In the Book of Revelation, there are listed the End-Time Seven Seals, The Seven Trumpets and The Seven Bowls of Wrath.

In the third event of the Seven Trumpets, the "Wormwood Star" falls from the sky and destroys all the drinking water and most of life. Some also call Nemesis the Wormwood Star.

Question here is (as some theologians and scientists conclude) does Almighty God release the Brown Dwarf Star whenever the people on Earth completely disobey His precepts and become totally unrighteous?

The Bad News

If either Planet X (called Nibiru) which is around 1.5 light years from the sun ... or PlanetTyche (called Hercolubus) --- which is about 2/3rd of a light year --- orbits the Sun, then we can expect an apocalyptic End Time devastation of Planet Earth.

Astronomers, scientists and theologians say, "This is not a matter of "if" but "when."

The Good News

As promised by Almighty God, His only begotten Son, Jesus Christ, will appear in the sky and His Holy Spirit will rapture up in safety to Heaven --- all who accepted Jesus as their Lord, King and Savior. And He does this before any distant planet or star hits earth. Praise God!

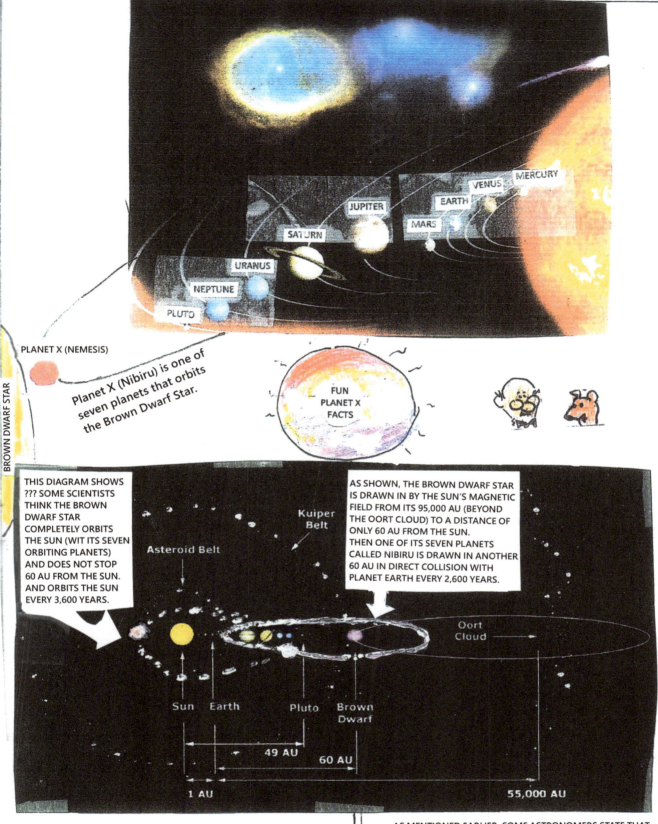

PLANET X (NEMESIS)

Planet X (Nibiru) is one of seven planets that orbits the Brown Dwarf Star.

FUN PLANET X FACTS

BROWN DWARF STAR

THIS DIAGRAM SHOWS ??? SOME SCIENTISTS THINK THE BROWN DWARF STAR COMPLETELY ORBITS THE SUN (WIT ITS SEVEN ORBITING PLANETS) AND DOES NOT STOP 60 AU FROM THE SUN. AND ORBITS THE SUN EVERY 3,600 YEARS.

AS SHOWN, THE BROWN DWARF STAR IS DRAWN IN BY THE SUN'S MAGNETIC FIELD FROM ITS 95,000 AU (BEYOND THE OORT CLOUD) TO A DISTANCE OF ONLY 60 AU FROM THE SUN. THEN ONE OF ITS SEVEN PLANETS CALLED NIBIRU IS DRAWN IN ANOTHER 60 AU IN DIRECT COLLISION WITH PLANET EARTH EVERY 2,600 YEARS.

THE BROWN DWARF STAR IS ABOUT 95,000 AU FROM THE SUN (BEYOND THE OORT CLOUD) AND THE SUN'S MAGNETIC FIELD PULLS IT WITH 60 AU OF IT.
ONE OF THE SEVEN PLANETS THAT ORBITS THE BROWN DWARF STAR (CALLED PLANET X OR NIBIRU) IS MAGNETICALLY PULLED ANOTHER 60 AU CLOSER TO THE SUN IN DIRECT COLLISION OF THE PLANET EARTH, WHICH POTENTIALLY OCCURS EVERY 2,600 YEARS.

AS MENTIONED EARLIER, SOME ASTRONOMERS STATE THAT THE BROWN DWARF STAR ORBITS COMPLETELY AROUND THE SUN EVERY 3,600 YEARS.
HOWVER, BOTH SIDES FIGURES THE BROWN DWARF STAR TO BE ABOUT 95,000 AU (OR ABOUT 1.5 LIGHT YEARS) FRM THE SUN.
ALL THIS MAY BE HYPOTHETICAL, BUT MORE AND MORE DATA FROM ASTRONOMERS WILL EVENTUALLY PROVE OR DISPROVE THE EXISTENCE OF THE BROWN DWARF STAR. SCIENTISTS DO, HOWEVER, SAY DESTRUCTION OF EARTH IS NOT IF BUT WHEN.

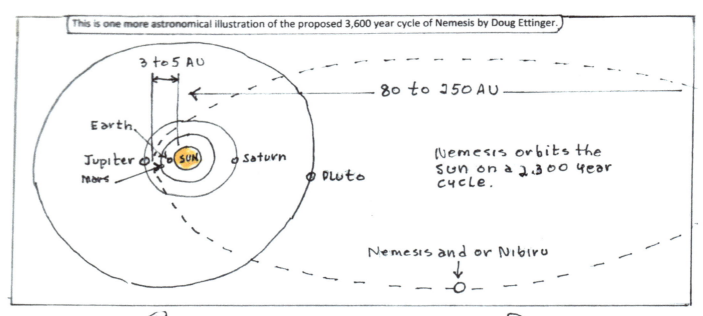

This is one more astronomical illustration of the proposed 3,600 year cycle of Nemesis by Doug Ettinger.

Shown below are pictures of the Brown Dwarf Star (Nemesis) and its orbiting Nibiru Planet which allegedly orbits our Sun every 2,160 years.

If Nemesis does pass even in the outer edges of our Solar System, it can disturb literally trillions of comets in the Oort Cloud --- which will plummet toward Jupiter, Saturn and even Earth.

This is a vivid picture of the Brown Dwarf Star as it is seen by an infrared telescope from a southern South Pole direction.
If Nemesis is too far away for an accurate confirmation of its existence, then another possible companion Sun might be "Tyche." It is only one-third of a light year away as opposed to Nemesis' 1.5 light years away.

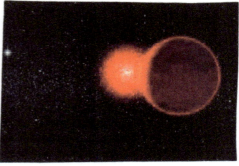

Nemesis is (at this point in time) a theoretical "Death Star" companion to the Sun. Nemesis has an alleged apocalyptic 2,160 year orbiting cycle around the Sun ... and (if it does exists) is about 1.5 light years from the Sun, but it is still within the Sun's gravitational pull

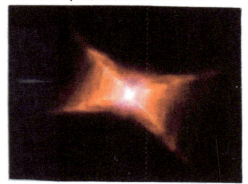

Nibiru and its moons (satellites) means the planet of the crossing. The Christ-like cross in the sky is considered by many theologians and astronomers as the sign of the End Times.

Many corporate and church type logos are analogues to the reddish type cross produced by Nibiru as is somewhat prophetically portrayed by the Holy Spirit of the United Methodist Cross.

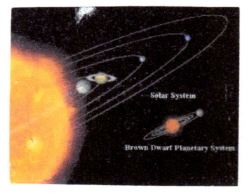

The Brown Dwarf Star (possibly 95,000 AU from our Sun) is also called Nemesis. It has 7 planets orbiting it --- and is 50 times the size of Jupiter.

SCRIPTURE 2 PETER 3:5-13 PEOPLE IGNORE THAT GOD COMMANDED HUMAN AND EARTH BE CREATED WHICH WAS FORMED BY WATER AND BY THE FLOOD OF WATER IT WAS DESTROYED. THE HEAVENS AND EARTH, WHICH NOW EXIST, WILL BE DESTROYED THIS TIME BY FIRE. THIS IS HOW THE GODLESS PEOPLE ON EARTH WILL BE JUDGED. AND THOSE WHO BELIEVE IN GOD'S ONLY BEGOTTEN SON, JESUS CHRIST, AS THEIR LORD, KING AND SAVIOR WILL BEFOREHAND BE RAPTURED UP INTO A NEW HEAVEN AND A NEW EARTH.

Shown below are the 8 Planets plus Pluto and their time to orbit the Sun.

"Planet X (has many name such as Brown Dwarf Star BDS, Nibiru, Planet 9, Second Sun, God's Judgment Star, Nemesis, Destroyer, Red Dragon Herco,umbus, Wormwood, to name a few.

Planets X is sent into our Solar System every 3,000 years or so, whenever humankind falls below the unrighteousness of Sodom $ Gomorrrah/

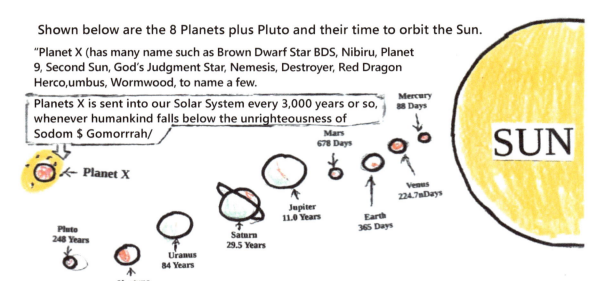

FUN PLANET X FACTS

PROS

IN 1991, ROBERT S HARINGTON, HEAD OF THE NAVAL OBSERVATION IN WASHINGTON, DC INVESTIGATED THE FACTS AND FICTION OF PLANET X.
HARRINGTON WAS CERTAIN HE HAD FOUND THE EXACT POSITION OF THE LARGE ROGUE PLANET X THAT WAS ENTERING OUR SOLAR SYSTEM ... AND REPORTED THAT ANYONE WHO DARED TO REPORT IT WAS THREATENED WITH FEAR OR EVEN DEATH.
SO A SHROUD OF DECEPTION AND POSSIBLE MURDER SURROUNDS THE EXPOSURE OF PLANET X.

PICTURE OF THE NAVAL OBSERVATORY

COUNTRIES AROUND THE WORLD ARE BUILDING UNDERGROUND BUNKERS FILLED WITH MEDICINE, FOOD AND OTHER SUPPLIES ... WHICH WILL DO LITTLE GOOD AS THE TIDAL WAVES AND UNDER THE EARTH WATER WILL FILL THE BUNKERS TO THE BRIM.
AND BACTERIA, MOLD AND OTHR DISEASES WILL AFFLICT MANY INSIDE.

CONS

ACCORDING TO RECENT REPORTS, NASA'S FIRST AFFIRMATION OF SEEING PLANET X WAS LATER DESCRIBED AS NOTHING MORE THAN DENSE GAS CLOUDS IN OUR ATMOSPHERE.

MOST PROBABLY THERE RE ARE MANY SCIENTISTS AS WELL AS ASTRONOMERS WHO DISBELIEVE THE EXISTENCE OF PLANET X (NIBIRU). AND HAVE PUT IT ON THE STAND-BY-AND-WAIT-AND SEE-SHELF.

AS SOME ASTRONOMERS SAY, "I'M SORRY ... BUT THE PLANET X DID NOT SHOW UP IN 2012 AND IT IS ALREADY 2014. SMELL THE COFFEE."

ACCORDING TO MANY REPORTERS, ALL THE DOOMSDAY HYPE ABOUT PLANET X WAS NOTHIING MORE THAN A MISLEADING SHAM TO SELL MORE BOOKS, CD'S AND OTHER PARAPHERNALIA.

Shown below are the 8 Planets plus Pluto and their time to orbit the Sun.

"Planet X (has many name such as Brown Dwarf Star BDS, Nibiru, Planet 9, Second Sun, God's Judgment Star, Nemesis, Destroyer, Red Dragon Herco,umbus, Wormwood, to name a few.

Planets X is sent into our Solar System every 3,000 years or so, whenever humankind falls below the unrighteousness of Sodom $ Gomorrrah/

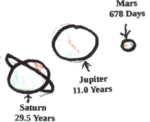
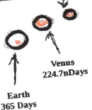

PROS

THE SCIENTIST, JAMES M. MCCANNEY, AFFIRMS THAT THE BROWN DWARF STAR AND ITS ACCOMPANYING PLANET X IS REAL.
ACCORDING TO JAMES M. MCCANNEY, WHO HAS DEALT WITH NASA DURING HIS CAREER, NASA IS UNDER STRICT CONGRESSIONAL ORDER NOT TO TELL ANYONE IF SUCH A ROGUE TYPE PLANET X COULD CAUSE WORLD-WIDE DESTRUCTION.

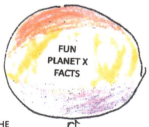

NASA FIRST ANNOUNCED PLANET X EXISTED IN THE 1980'S AS REPORTED IN THE JUNE 19, 1982 EDITION OF THE NEW YORK TIMES.

WITHIN A WEEK'S TIME, NASA RETRACTED THE STORY IN THE NEW YORK TIMES ... BUT THERE IS INTERNAL EVIDENCE THAT NASA IS STILL TRACKING THE BROWN DWARF STAR AND ITS ORBITING PLANET X.

SOME SCIENTISTS HAVE CLAIMED THE BROWN DWARF STAR AS THE BINARY STAR TO OUR SUN.

NASA HAS ALLEGEDLY BEEN AWARE OF THE BROWN DWARF STAR FOR THE PAST 30 YEARS.

ACCORDING TO SOME ASSTRONOMERS, THE BROWN DWARF STAR AND ITS ORBITING 7 PLANETS IS FAST CLOSING IN ON UNSUSPECTING EARTH WITH ITS I METEORITES, COMETS, RED DUST AND VIOLENT WINDS.

CONS

MANY SAY THAT THE PICTURES OF THE BROWN DWARF STAR AND ITS 7 ORBITING PLANETS ARE OUTRIGHT FAKES OR MISINTERPRETATIONS OR PHOTO MANIPULATIONS.

IN 1995, NANCY LIEDER, FOUNDER OF THE WEBSITE ZETA TALK' SAID SHE RECEIVED EXTRA-TERRESTRIAL TRANSMITTALS FROM AN IMPLANT PLACED INSIDE HER BRAIN. MANY HAVE SUBSSCRIBED HER AS BEING A VERY MISLEADING PROPHETESS. BUT WHO KNOWS FOR SURE AS MANY HUMANS HAVE HAD STRANGE IMPLANTS SURGICALLY REMOVED FROM THERE BODIES.,

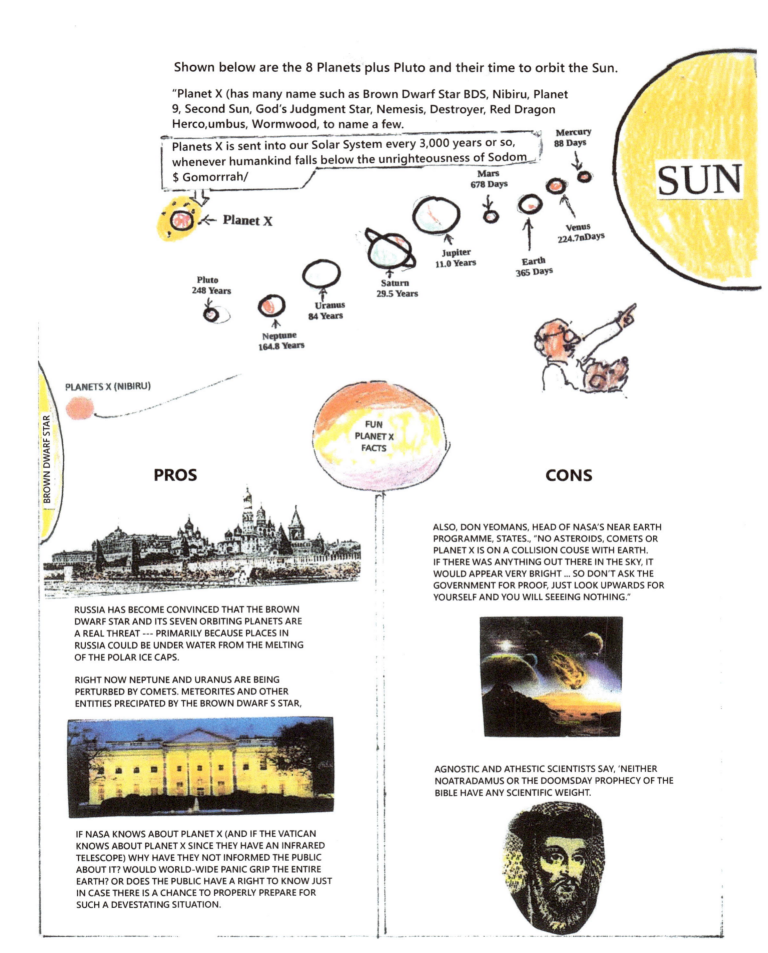

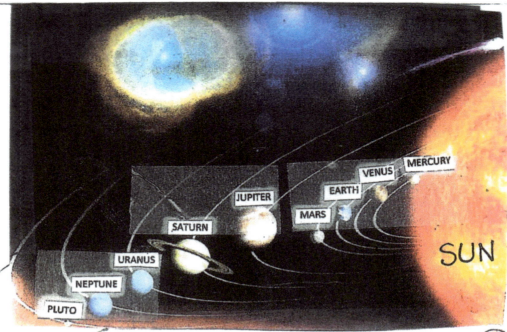

PLANET X (NIBIRU)

BROWN DWAFR STAR

FUN PLANET X FACTS

PROS

THE BROWN DWARF STAR'S, BDS, ELYPTICAL ORBIT AROUND THE SUN IS EVERY 2,100 YEARS ... AND ITS SECOND 2,100 ORBIT CAN CAUSE EVEN MORE APOCALYPTIC DESTRUCTION ON EARTH.
THE BROWN DWARF STAR IS ABOUT 1.5 LIGHT YEARS FROM THE SUN (JUST OUTSIDE OUR SOLAR SYSTEM) BUT IT IS STILL WITHIN THE GRAVITATIONAL PULL OF THE SUN. SOME ASTRONOMERS AND SCIENTISTS NOW BELIEVE THE BDS (ASO CALLED PLANET X) IS NOW PULLED INSIDE OUR SOLAR SYSTEM CAUSING THE UNUSUAL BAD WEATHER OF HEAVY RAINS AND LIGHTNING, FLOODS, TSUNAMIS, HURICANES, VOLCANOES, TORNADOES AND EARTHQUAKES.

SOME ASTRONOMERS CONCLUDE THAT THE BROWN DWARF STAR COMES ONLY WITHIN 60 AU OF THE SUN AND THEN ONE OF ITS SEVEN ORBITING PLANETS (CALLED NEMESIS) ORBITS ANOTHER 60 AU DIRECTLY IN LINE WITH THE ORBIT OF PLANET EARTH. THAT WILL CAUSE LESS DESTRUCTION IF PLANET EARTH'S ORBIT IS ON THE OTHER SIDE OF THE SUN AT THAT SPECIFIC TIME.

HOWEVER, IF THE BROWN DWARF STAR (CALLED SO AS IT DOES NOT HAVE THE BRIGHT FUSION OF THE SUN) ---BUT (ITS DIAMETER IS ABOUT 40% THE SIZE OF THE SUN) ORBITS COMPLETELY AROIUND THE SUN, THEN IT WILL CAUSE TREMENDOUS DESTRUCTION TO EARTH'S POLARIZATION WHICH WILL HAVE EVEN CONTINENTS (WHICH ARE LAYERS OF LAND ON TOP OF MAGNA) SWISH AROUND AND FLIP FLOPPING THEM WHEREBY THE ANTARCTICA MIGHT BE UP NEAR AFRICA AND MAINE CAN VERY WELL BE SWIRLED INTO THE VICINITY OF FLORIDA.

CONS

DR. PETER EISENHARDT. A SCIENTISTS FOR THE MISSION AT NASA JET PROPULSION LABORATORY IN PASADENA, CA., SAID, 'WE KNOW THAT THERE ARE MORE BROWN STARS IN OUR SOLAR SYSTEM AND MILKY WAY GALAXY THAN THERE ARE REGULAR STARS LIKE OUR SUN. MANY OF THE BROWN DWARF STARS ARE ALMOST INVISIBLE EVEN TO THE INFRARED TELESCOPES.'

IN 1989, NASA'S VOYAGE 2 ESTABLISHED THAT NO REAL IRREGULARITY OR PERTURBATIONS WERE OCCURING. ON NEPTUNE OR URANUS.

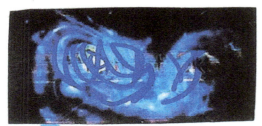

PLANET X (NIBIRU)

BROWN DWARF STAR

FUN PLANET X FACTS

PROS

THE BROWN DWARF STAR (WITH ITS 7 PLANETS OF WHICH ONE IS NAMED "NEMESIS" AND IS ALSO VISIBLE EVERY 2,160 YEARS VIEWED MOSTLY FROM A SOUTHERN DIRECTION.

RECENT CALCULATIONS THE NAVAL OBSERVATORY CONFIRMS THAT HABITUAL PERTURBANCE OF URANUS AND NEPTUNE WHICH DR. THOMAS C VAN FLANDORN, AN ASTRONOMER, SAYS THIS COULD BE CAUSED BY A SINGULAR ELLIPTICAL ORBITING PLANET POSSIBLY 5 TIMES THE SIZE OF EARTH WHICH MAY BE 5 BILLION MILES BEYOND PLUTO ... BUT STILL WITHIIN THE GRAVATICAL INFUENCE OF THE SUN."

ON SEPTEMBER 10, 1984 THE 'US NEWS & WORLD REPORT" MAGAZINE STATED THAT THE INFRARED ASTRONOMICAL SATELLITE (IRAS), WHILE CIRCLING A POLAR ORBIT ABOUT 560 MILES FROM THE EARTH, DETECTED HEAT FROM AN OBJECT 50 BILLION MILES AWAY AND WAS PUT UNDER INVESTIGATION.

THE SUN IS AT AN EXCITED LEVEL AS IT IS GIVING OFF MORE SOLAR FLARES.

SOME SCIENTISTS SAY, THAT THE EVENTUAL COMING OF THE BROWN DWARF STAR AND ITS ORBITING SEVEN PLANETS IS NOT A MATTER OF "IF" .... BUT "WHEN!"

CONS

THE HYPOTHESIS OF PLANET X (NIBIRU) STARTED BY EXAMINING THE 2900-1800 BC CLAY TABLETS OF THE SUMERIANS WICH FEATURED THE ORBITING PLANETS OF THE SUN BUT LISTED ELEVEN PLANETS (NOT JUST 9).

ACCORDING TO SOME HISTORIANS, ZECHARIA SITCHIN TOOK COMPLETE ADVANTAGE OF MAKING MORE FICTION THAN FACT ABOUT THE SUMERIAN CLAY TABLETS. HIS BOOK WHICH NAMED THE PLANET INHABITANTS "THE ANNUNAKIS' ALSO MADE HIS BOOK A BEST SELLER.

MANY SCIENTISTS REPORTEDLY THINK THAT THE MAYAN CALENDAR IS NOTHING MORE THAN A MYTH.

Shown below are the 8 Planets plus Pluto and their time to orbit the Sun.

"Planet X (has many name such as Brown Dwarf Star BDS, Nibiru, Planet 9, Second Sun, God's Judgment Star, Nemesis, Destroyer, Red Dragon Herco,umbus, Wormwood, to name a few.

Planets X is sent into our Solar System every 3,000 years or so, whenever humankind falls below the unrighteousness of Sodom $ Gomorrrah/

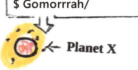 ← Planet X

 SUN

Mercury 88 Days
Mars 678 Days
Venus 224.7nDays
Earth 365 Days
Jupiter 11.0 Years
Saturn 29.5 Years
Uranus 84 Years
Neptune 164.8 Years
Pluto 248 Years

PLANET X (NIBIRU)

BROWN DWARF STAR

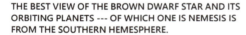 FUN PLANET X FACTS

PROS

PLANET X IS VERY DIFFICULT FOR AN AMATEUR ASTRONOMER TO DETECT AS IT IS SO BRIGHT AND BECAUSE OF ITS SKEWED ELLYPTICAL ORBIT. ALTHOUGH IT CAN BE SEEN, AT TIMES, IN THE SPRING FROM A SOUTH POLE DIRECTION.

THE BEST VIEW OF THE BROWN DWARF STAR AND ITS ORBITING PLANETS --- OF WHICH ONE IS NEMESIS IS FROM THE SOUTHERN HEMESPHERE.

THE BROWN DWARF STAR (ALSO CALLED PLANET X) IS MANY TIMES HIDDEN BY THE SUN'S GLARE, BUT CAN BE SEEN SOME TIMES AT MIDDAY WHEN THE CLOUDS BLOCK THE SUN'S RAYS.

IN CHAPTER 8 OF THE BOOK OF REVELATION IN THE BIBLE, IT EXPLAINS WHERE A METEROID STORM AND THE WORMWOOD STAR FALL UPON THE EARTH AND TURNS THE WATER TO BITTERNESS AND BLOOD CAUSING MANY TO DIE.

THE VELOCITY OF PLANET X CAN CAUSE SUCH A SHAKING OF THE EARTH THAT FROM THE GROUND WILL APPEAR BUGS, SNAKES AND OTHER VARMITS.

CONS

PRESENTLY, HOWEVER, WHILE THE SCIENTISTS SAY THAT PLANET X IS ON THE SHELF OF POSSIBLE NONEXISTENCE, THEY ARE SEEKING INFORMATION ABOUT "HERCOLUBUS" SUPPOSEDLY A PLANET 6 TIMES BIGGER THAN THE PLANET JUPITER.

THE PLANET HERCOLUBUS BELONGS IN THE SOLAR SYSTEM OF TYLO. IT IS RAPIDLY APPROACHING OUR SOLAR SYSTEM, WHICH CAN CAUSE DEVASTATING CONSEQUENCES FOR PLANET EARTH.

ACCORDING TO DR. JOHN CARSON, DIRECTOR OF THE CENTER FOR ARCHAEOASTRONOMY, THE MAYAN CALENDAR PROPHECY OF AN APOCALYPTIC EVENT IN 2012 WAS A MISCONCEPTION FROM THE VERY BEGINNING.

Shown below are the 8 Planets plus Pluto and their time to orbit the Sun.

"Planet X (has many name such as Brown Dwarf Star BDS, Nibiru, Planet 9, Second Sun, God's Judgment Star, Nemesis, Destroyer, Red Dragon Herco,umbus, Wormwood, to name a few.

Planets X is sent into our Solar System every 3,000 years or so, whenever humankind falls below the unrighteousness of Sodom $ Gomorrrah/

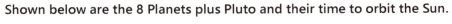
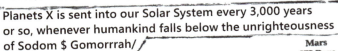

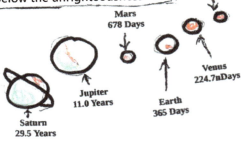

← Planet X

Mercury 88 Days
SUN
Mars 678 Days
Venus 224.7nDays
Jupiter 11.0 Years
Earth 365 Days
Saturn 29.5 Years
Uranus 84 Years
Neptune 164.8 Years
Pluto 248 Years

PLANET X (NIBIRU)
BROWN DWARF STAR

PROS

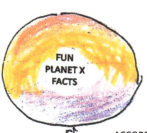

FUN PLANET X FACTS

CONS

THERE IS NO DELAY IN THE LORD GOD'S ETERNAL JUDGEMENT OF THE GODLESS. HE IS JUST HOLDING BACK UNTIL THE COMPLETE NUMBER OF PEOPLE CAN BE SAVED.

MANY WILL SAY, 'HOW AND WHY CAN GOD BE SO MERCIFULESS TO THOSE WHO ARE LEFT ON EARTH. AND HIS ANSWER IS, 'BECAUSE THAT IS HOW THEY TREATED MY PEOPLE AND TURNED TO THE DARKNESS OF THE EVIL DEMONS.
IT IS AT THIS TIME ALSO, THAT SATAN, THE BEAST AND ANTICHRIST ARE ALL TOSSED INTO THE PIT OF FIRE AND SULFUR.

ACCORDING TO SOME SCIENTISTS, THE HERCOLUBUS STAR IS POSSIBLY THE BROWN DWARF STAR. THE HERCOLUMBUS STAR IS 600 TIMES THE SIZE OF THE EARTH. SOME SCIENTISTS CALL THE HERCOLUBUS STAR THE BIBLICAL STAR NAMED THE WORMWOOD STAR THAT PLUMETS THE EARTH AT THE END TIME.
BUT THIS IS HALFHEARTED BELIEF OF MANY SCIENTISTS.

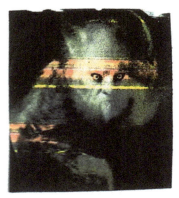

FROM THE VIEWPOINT OF THEOLOGIANS AND SOME SCIENTISTS, ABOUT EVERY 4,000+ YEARS,
THE HUMANS ON EARTH TURN AWAY FROM GOD AND FOLLOW THE DARKNESS OF THE EVIL SPIRITS (FALLEN ANGELS).
THE PEOPLE OF THE EARTH SAY, "WHERE IS GOD?" WITHOUT REALIZING THAT 1,000 YEARS OF MANKIND IS BUT ONE DAY TO THE LORD GOD.
SO IN EXCHANGE, THE PEOPLE TURN TO EVIL THOUGHTS, DOUBTS, AND NONREPENTANCE.

SOME SCIENTISTS SAY THAT THE MAYAN, HOPNI, EGYPTIAN AS WELL AS THE WORMWOOD STAR ARE SCARE TACTICS TO AGAIN SELL MORE BOOKS, CD'S AND BEGIN A LANDSLIDE OF NEW BROWN STAR TPE CONSPIRACIES.

Shown below are the 8 Planets plus Pluto and their time to orbit the Sun.

"Planet X (has many name such as Brown Dwarf Star BDS, Nibiru, Planet 9, Second Sun, God's Judgment Star, Nemesis, Destroyer, Red Dragon Herco,umbus, Wormwood, to name a few.

Planets X is sent into our Solar System every 3,000 years or so, whenever humankind falls below the unrighteousness of Sodom $ Gomorrrah/

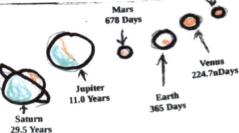

Mercury 88 Days
Mars 678 Days
Venus 224.7nDays
Jupiter 11.0 Years
Earth 365 Days
Pluto 248 Years
Neptune 164.8 Years
Uranus 84 Years
Saturn 29.5 Years
Planet X

PROS

BROWN DWARF STAR
PLANET X (NIBIRU)

MANY THEOLOGIANS AS WELL AS SCIENTISTS SAY THAT THE LORD GOD IS HOLDING BACK THE ORBIT OF THE BROWN DWARF STAR (ALSO CALLED PLANET X) AND ITS SEVEN ORBITING PLANETS UNTIL THE VERY LAST PERSON CAN BE SAVED.
THIS SALVATION, ACCORDING TO SCRIPTURE, ARE THOSE WHO ACCEPT GOD'S ONLY BEGOTTEN SON, JESUS CHHRIST, AS THEIR LORD, KING AND SAVIOR.
AND THEY ARE RAPTURED BY THE HOLY SPIRIT OF GOD BEFORE THE PLANET X ORBITS EARTH CAUSING THE JUDGEMENT OF THE GODLESS.

FUN PLANET X FACTS

CONS

IN 1976, ZECHARIAH SITCHIN, A THEORETICAL ASTRONOMER PROCLAIMED THAT PLANET X (NIBIRU) WAS RECORDED ON ANCIENT BABYLONIAN TEXTS. SITCHIN CALLED THE INHABITANTS OF PLANET X THE ANNUNAKI WHO ALLEGEDLY WERE THE FIRST SPACE ALIENS TO VISIT THE SUMERIAN TRIBE.
AGAIN, MANY HUMANS HAVE REPORTED SEEING AND BEING TAKEN UP BY SPACE ALIEN UFO'S SO WHO IS TO SAY, AS OF YET, --- TRUE OR FALSE.

IT IS YOUR CHOICE. WOULD YOU RATHER HAVE
THE JUDGMENT OR THE RAPTURE

AFTER THE RAPTURE, THERE WILL BE THREE AND A HALF YEARS OF PEACE AND THEN ALL HADES BREAKS LOOSE. SATAN BECOMES MORE THAN EVER PARANOID ABOUT BEING BETRAYED, AND HE HAS THE INFAMOUS 666 PLACED ON THE PEOPLE'S FOREHEAD OR HAND...
AS HE KNOWS THAT ANYONE WITH THE 666 MARK CANNOT EVER GET INTO HEAVEN.
THEN WARS AND RUMORS OF WARS PLAGUE THE WORLD WITH DEMONS CAUSING PANIC AND WIDE SPREAD TERROR.
FINALLY ALMIGHTY GOD TOSSES SATAN THE BEAST AND THE ANTICHRIST INTO THE PIT OF FIRE AND SULFUR.

QUESTION: WHY??? IF YOU TYPE IN THE COORDINATES IN GOOGLE 5TH 53M 27 -6 10' 58 IT IS BLOCKED OUT FROM SEEING THE ORION ARM OF THE MILKY WAY.
THAT IS WHERE OUR SOLAR SYSTEM IS LOCATED. IS SOMEONE BLOCKING THIS PORTION OF THE SKY SO NO POSSIBLE DEVASTATING CONSEQUENCES OF EARTH CAN BE SEEN. PLEASE KEEP IN MIND THIS IS JUST A QUESTION. NOT A PRO OR CON OF PLANET X OR THE BROWN DWARF STAR.

WE JUST WONDER, "WHY?"

HERE IS AN OUTLINE OF WHAT YOU READ SO FAR.

TOPIC **EXPLANATION** **PAGE**

(1) **PLANET X IS ALSO CALLED THE BROWN DWARF STAR (BDS):** On page 48 it show the orbit of Planet X. The collision problem will occur if Planet X (which orbits the Sun clockwise) and the Earthly Planets (orbit the Sun counterclockwise wise). If that happens the Earth's Tectonic Plates will be jerked hundreds and even thousands of miles apart. The end result will be the thousands of volcanoes on Planet Earth will explode, and the smoke and fire will make the Sun turn black, the Moon to lose its light and the asteroids between Mars and Jupiter will catastrophically plummet the Earth into massive destruction. Planet X exists right outside our Solar System, but when Humankind exceeds the unrighteous of Sodom & Gomorrah, the Almighty God sends forth Planet X into our Solar System (around 2,300 years or so) as punishment of our not repenting of our Sodom-Gomorrah type sins. In Matthew, 24:29, The Disciples asked Jesus, "What will happen at the End time?" Jesus prophesied, to them, "The Sun will turn turn black, the moon will lose its light, and the stars in the Heavens will plummet the Earth." 47

(2) **VISUAL OF THE END TIMES:** This displays a visual of the many things that will happen at the END TIME, and how Jesus will rapture the "Born Again" Judaeo-Christians into Heaven before the apocalypse occurs on Earth.................48

(3) **A PICTORIAL OF THE PLANETS --- AND FACTS ABOUT PLANET X:** This page shows all of the 9 Planets and how Planets X lies just outside of our Solar system ... and how it enters our solar system and can cause minimal destruction or total Earth destruction if it completely orbits our Sun.................49

(4) **VARIOUS ACTUAL PICTURES OF PLANET X:** These are pictures ken by the Infrared Telescope. Another name for Planet X is a "Christ Like Crossing" in the sky.................50

(5) **THE PROS AND CONS OF PLANET X EXISTENCE:** a PRO is Robert S. Harrington (Head of the Naval Observation in Washington, D. C. traveled to Iceland and logged the fact that Planet X existed .... but was found dead not long afterwards/ The CON is the Governmental Scientist say that Planet X is a sham to sell books. You decide yourself 51

(6) More **PROS and CONS OF Planet X FOR YOU TO ANALYZE:** a PRO is James M, McCanney (who has dealt with NASA) and is under strict orders not to discuss anything about Planet X. NASA is reportedly tracking to confirm Planet X. Some reports from other scientists is that Planet X is causing unusual and harsh weather conditions. The CON is that pictures of Planet X are fakes.................53.

(7) **RUSSIA BELIEVES IN THE EXISTENCE OF PLANET X:** A PRO is that Russia has underground bunkers for protection from Nuclear Attack and Planet X. A CON is some NASA scientist say, "Planets X and Nostradamus have no scientific weight.................54

(8) **IS PLANET X REALLY NOW INSIDE OUR SOLAR SYSTEM:** A PRO is that the Antarctic (when dug deep) scientists find remains of Palm Trees and African like elephants. The CON is that NASA states that there are Brown Dwarf Stars in other Solar Systems, but none in our Solar System...55

(9) **THE SUN IS SHEDDING MORE SOLAR FLARES:** As A PRO Scientific believers say, "The eventual arrival of Planet X is not a matter of 'if ... but when." As a CON is that Zecharia Sitchin (a Russian Scientist) wrote about Planet X just to make money 56

(10) **IF PLANET X SHAKES EARTH VARIOUS VARMINTS APPEAR:** A PRO is that the Book of Revelation explains where at the END TIME various varmints will arise out of the Earth. A CON is that previous descriptions such as the Mayan Calendar is a misconception of the END TIME..57

(11) **ACCORDING TO BELIEVERS EVERY 4,000 YEARS IS BAD:** As a PRO, some Theologians say, "Every 4,000 years humankind turns evil and God rectifies it with Planet X every 2,300 years, As a CON, the nonbelievers say it is just a ploy to sell more books and videos...58

(12) **GOD SLOW DOWN PLANET X TO SHOW SIGNS OF END TIME:** At the End Time, Satan has seven years of domain in which the first 3 ½ years are blissful, but he next 3 ½ years will be excruciatingly bad as Satan's paranoia puts the infamous 666 number of peoples forehead or hand in order to buy food. Which makes one wonder what his happening in the Orion Arm of our Milky Way Galaxy 59

AFFIRMATION OF PLANET X

FACING THE PEOPLE AND FACTS ABOUT PLANET X

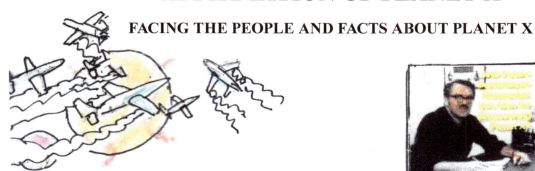

THERE ARE APPROXIMATELY 500 MILITARY PLANES KC-125 TANKERS PAINTED WHITE TO LOOK LIKE THE CIVILIAN AIRLINES. THESE MILITARY PLANES ARE SPREADING CHEMTRAILS CONSISTING OF BARIUM, ALUMINUM AND MANY OTHER TOXIC CHEMICALS INTO THE SKY WHICH FALL TO EARTH POLLUTING THE EARTH'S WATER, SOIL CROPS, FOOD AND THE HUMANS THEMSELVES.
THE BARIUM IS VERY HEAVY IN THE CLOUDS AND EVENTUALLY WEIGHS SO MUCH THAT FLOODS, HURRICANES AND TORNADOES ARE ITS AFTERMATH IN ESSENCE, THE CHEMICALS IN THE CHEMTRAILS CAN CAUSE DISEASES IN A HUMAN'S HEAD, CHEST, STOMACH AND IMMUNE SYSTEM.
THE GOVERNMENTAL AND COMPANY RATIONAL TO SPRAY THE CHEMTRAILS IS BECAUSE THE SUN IS EMITTING TREMENDOUSLY STRONG SOLAR FLARES PRODUCING VERY HIGH RADIATION LEVELS. WORD HAS IT THAT PLANET X IS NOW INSIDE OUR SOLAR SYSTEM AND CAUSING BOTH THE SUN AND EARTH'S MAGNETIC FIELD TO FALTER AND BE PERTURBED. THE EARTH ITSELF HAS TILTED MORE THAN USUAL AND THE INNER AND LIQUID CORE IN BOTH THE SUN AND EARTH ARE ALSO DISTURBED. SINCE 1975 THERE HAS BEEN A 500 PERCENT INCREASE IN VOLCANO AND EARTHQUAKE OCCURRENCES. THESE ARE DEFINITE "SIGNS" OF PLANET X DOING ALL THIS.
ONCE AGAIN, THE PROTECTION FROM ALL OF THIS IS **"DON'T BE SCARED, JUST GET PREPARED."** THIS IS ACCOMPLISHED BY TRULY REPENTING OF YOUR SINS, ACCEPTING JESUS (YESHUA) AS YOU LORD AND SAVIOR, AND ASKING FOR HIS HOLY SPIRIT TO RAISE YOU UP --- IF AND WHEN PLANET X DOES DESTRUCTIVELY ORBIT OUR SUN.

ROBERT S. HARRINGTON, THE HEAD OF THE NAVAL OBSERVATORY IN WASHINGTON, D. C. PERSONALLY FLEW TO NEW ZEALAND TO DOCUMENT THE EXISTENCE OF PLANET X. IN DOING SO, HE FOUND THE EXACT COORDINATES OF PLANET X, WHICH IS IS A MINIATURE SUN, BUT IT DOES NOT HAVE THE FUSION CAPABILITY OF OUR REGULAR SUN.
HARRINGTON TRACKED PLANET X WHICH IS ALSO CALLED THE BROWN DWARF STAR AND ITS PATH OF EVENTUALLY DESTRUCTIVELY ORBITING OUR SUN … SINCE IT IS WITH THE GRAVITATIONAL PULL OF OUR SUN EVERY 2,160 YEARS TO AS MUCH AS EVERY 3,700 YEARS.
HOWEVER, MANY ASTRONOMERS AND SCIENTISTS THINK PLANET X IS OVERDUE IN ITS ARRIVAL.
AFTER MAKING HIS REPORT, ROBERT S. HARRINGTON, WHO WAS SUPPOSEDLY IN GOOD HEALTH, MYSTERIOUSLY DIED, WHICH MANY FEEL HE WAS MURDERED. ADD TO THAT IS THE FACT THAT ABOUT 40 ASTRONOMERS MYSTERIOUSLY DIED WHO WERE TRACKING PLANET X.

GADS, THIS IS GETTING SPOOKY.

I UNDERSTAND THAT ABOUT 40 40 ASTRONOMERS ALSO MYSTERIOUSLY DIED WHO WERE TRACKING PLANET X. AND … ABOUT THERE WERE ABOUT 10 MICROBIOLOGIST WHO WERE TRACKING THE CHEMTRAILS ALSO DIED MYSTERIOUSLY.
QUESTION IS --- WHO IS MURDERING ALL OF THESE SCIENTISTS?

Many believers of Planet X find additional affirmation from Planet X Physicist, Claudia Albers and Space Photographer Scott C'one who tie scriptures in with planet and people events.

AFFIRMATION OF PLANET X

NOTE: The priests of the Catholic Church are working diligently to put a stop on all immoral and spiritual wrongs.

MALACHI MARTIN WAS A JESUIT PRIEST WHO LEFT THE JESUIT ORDER OF St IGNATIUS OF LOYOLA BECAUSE HE FOUND THEM TO BECOMING TOO SECULAR IN THEIR BELIEF.

THE JESUIT ORDER THEN RELIEVED MALACHI OF HIS JESUIT VOWS OF --- POVERTY, CHASITY AND OBEDIENCE TO GOD.

MALACHI ALSO MADE STRONG REFERENCE OF ALL **THE SATANIC RITUALS TAKING PLACE INSIDE THE VATICAN** --- INCLUDING PEDOPHILE, HOMO-SEXUALITY, APOSTASY AMONG A STRONG GROUP OF PRIESTS WHO DISBELIEVED IN SERVING CHRIST AND INSTEAD BEGAN SERVING SATAN.

MALACHI KNEW ABOUT THE ALIEN LIKE BEINGS WHO HAD A MEETING WITH FORMER PRESIDENT EISENHOWER AND A MEMBER OF THE VATICAN. ... AS WELL AS LIEN MEETINGS INSIDE THE VATICAN WHERE THE HUMANOIDS SUGGESTED THAT A ONE WORLD ORDER WAS NEEDED TO BEST SERVE THE NEEDS OF THE GLOBAL UNIVERSE.

MALACHI'S (SPIRIT OF DISCERNMENT) KNEW THAT THE ALIENS WERE NOTHING MORE THAN DEMONIC HUMANOID EMISSARIES OF THE DEVIL DECEIVING THE GOVERNMENT, THE VATICAN, THE MILITARY AND OTHER LEADERS INTO THE **SATANIC ONE WORLD ORDER.**

MALACHI HAD ACCESS TO THE JESUIT'S INFRARED TELESCOPE AND KNEW THAT PLANET X WAS REAL AND WAS IN DIRECT RELATIONSHIP WITH **THE THIRD SECRET OF FATIMA.** WHERE THE VATICAN WOULD BE INFILTRATED BY RUSSIAN AS WELL AS DEMONIC ACTIVITY. THUS HE WAS OSTRACIZED AND POSSIBLY EVEN MURDERED BECAUSE OF HIS SPIRITUAL INSIGHT.

MALACHI (JULY 13, 1921- JULY 27, 1999) WAS BORN IN IRELAND AND RECEIVED HIS DOCTORATES IN SEMITIC LANGUAGES, ARCHAEOLOGY AND ORIENTAL HISTORY ALONG WITH A PALEOGRAPHY DEGREE FROM THE CATHOLIC UNIVERSITY IN BLEGIUM; AND ALSO WAS A STUDENT AT OXFORD. MALACHI WOULD AGREE IN RELATION TO THE SAYING, **"DON'T BE SCARED, JUST GET PREPARED."** BY (1 REPENTING ... NOT JUST BEING SORRY, BUT CHANGING YOUR LIFESTYLE, (2) ACCEPT JESUS (YESHUA) AS YOUR LORD AND SAVIOR AND (3) ASKING FOR GOD'S HOLY SPIRIT THAT RAISED JESUS FROM THE DEAD AND WILL RAPTURE YOU TO HEAVEN IF AND WHEN PLANET X RAVISHLY ORBITS OUR SUN.

THE JESUITS OF THE CATHOLIC CHURCH HAVE AN INFRARED TELESCOPE (LOCATED IN ARIZONA) AND IT IS POINTED TOWARD THE SOUTHERN HEMISPHERE FROM WHICH PLANET X IS ON ITS WAY TO DESTRUCTIVELY ORBIT THE SUN AND DESTROY MOST OF THE EARTH AND ITS INHABITANTS.

PLANET X IS CALLED "THE SECOND EVIL SUN" BUT IT IS ALSO CALLED "GOD'S JUDGMENT STAR."

WORD IS THAT THE "JUDGMENT STAR" IS SENT BY ALMIGHTY GOD BECAUSE THE HUMAN RACE HAS FALLEN EVEN BELOW THE UNRIGHTEOUSNESS OF SODOM AND GOMORRAH.

THE NAME "SECOND EVIL SUN" IS UPON THOSE WHO SERVE SATAN RATHER THAN SERVING JESUS (YESHUA).

POPE JOHN PAUL II USED TO PEER THROUGH THE JESUIT INFRARED TELESCOPE AND ANNOUNCED THAT THERE WAS A DIRECT CONNECTION TO PLANET X AND THE THIRD SECRET OF FATIMA.

THERE IS SPECULATION THAT PLANET X IS CAUSING THE SUN TO EMIT SOLAR FLARES THAT ARE CAUSING THE MIDWEST TORNADOES AND FLOODS ... AND THE SECRET TYPE PLANES ARE SPRAYING CHEMTRAILS THAT ALSO CAUSE FLOODS.

THE LORD GOD STATES, 'IF I DO NOT INTERVENE AT THE END TIME, EVEN THE VERY ELECT WILL BE DECEIVED."

IN THE BOOK OF MATTHEW 24:29, WHEN THE DISCIPLES ASKED JESUS, "WHAT WILL HAPPEN AT THE END TIME"

JESUS REPLIED, 'AT THE END TIME, THE SUN WILL TURN BLACK, THE MOON WILL LOSE ITS LIGHT AND THE STARS WILL FALL FROM HEAVEN."

AND THAT, MY FRIENDS, WILL BE THE RESULT OF PLANET X SETTING OFF THE RING OF FIRE OF VOLCANOES.

PLANET X PHYSICISTS, DR. CLAUDIA MARTIN PROVIDES FURTHER SCIENTIFIC AFFIRMATION ABOUT PLANET X ALONG WITH SPACE PHOTOGRAPHER C'ONE

AFFIRMATION OF PLANET X

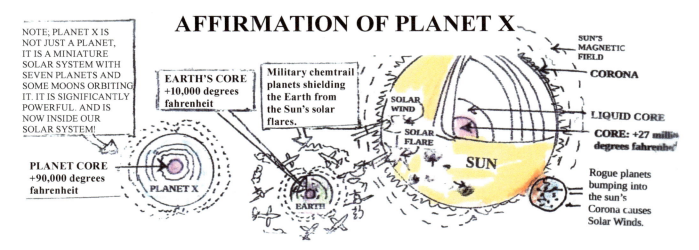

(1) PLANET X IS NOT JUST A PLANET, **IT IS A MINIATURE SOLAR SYSTEM** WITH SEVEN PLANETS ORBITING IT AND VARIOUS MOONS.

(2) **PLANET X IS NOW INSIDE OUR SOLAR SYSTEM** AND IT HAS CAUSE THE EARTH TO TILT PAST ITS NORMAL TILT OF 23.5 DEGREES WHICH HAS BROUGHT LESS WATER IN AREAS LIKE CAPETOWN AFRICA --- AND OTHER SHORE LINES.

(3) PLANET X MAKES THE **SUN'S MAGNETIC FIELD LINES TOUCH EACH OTHER** WHICH SHOOTS OUT "**SOLAR FLARES**" FROM THE SUN UPON EARTH. IT IS LIKE TWO ELECTRICAL LINES TOUCHING.

(4) PLANET X HAS LOOSEN SOME **DEAD STARS WHICH ARE PUSHING AGAINST THE SUN'S CORONA** WHICH CAUSE THE SUN TO SHOOT OFF "SOLAR WIND" UPON THE EARTH.

(5) MILITARY PLANES ARE FLYING AROUND THE EARTH EMITTING "**CHEMTRAILS**" WHICH IS A SMOKE LIKE CHEMICAL TRAIL CONSISTING OF BARIUM, ALUMINUM AND OTHER DANGEROUS CHEMICALS TO HUMAN, ANIMAL, BIRD, REPTILE, FISH AND INSECT LIFE. THE CHEMTRAILS CAN AND OFTEN DO CAUSE TREMENDOUS FLOODS.

(6) THEOLOGICAL ASTRONAUTS NAMES PLANET X "**GOD'S JUDGMENT STAR**" AS THE GLOBAL WORLD HAS NOW FALLEN BELOW THE UNRIGHTEOUSNESS OF SODOM 7 GOMORRAH. PLANET X WAS PRESENTED AS THE PLANET THAT DESTROYED THE SUMERIANS, ATLANTIS, THE MAYANS, NOAH'S ARK AND SODOM 7 GOMORRAH WHEN THEY FELL BELOW GOD'S PRECEPTS.

(7) IF YOU DO BELIEVE, THEN **DON'T BE SCARED, JUST GET PREPARED** BY --- (A) REPENTING OF YOUR SINS, (B ACCEPT JESUS AS YOUR SAVIOR (THE ISRAELITE CALL HIM YESHUA), © ASK FOR THE LORD GOD'S HOLY SPIRIT WHO WILL RAPTURE YOU IF AND WHEN PLANET X APOCALYPTICALLY ORBITS OUR SUN. GOT IT? OKAY, THEN TELL OTHERS AS IT WILL COVER A MULTITUDE OF YOUR OWN SINS. IN DOING SO.

(8) YOU DECIDE IF THE ABOVE INFORMATION IS SCIENCE, RELIGION FACT OR FICTION.

AFFIRMATION OF PLANET X

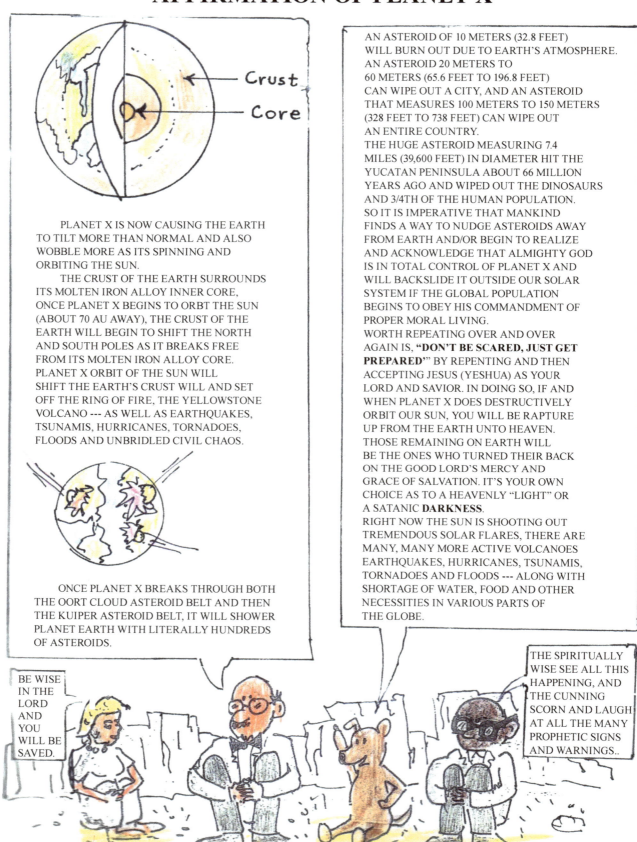

PLANET X IS NOW CAUSING THE EARTH TO TILT MORE THAN NORMAL AND ALSO WOBBLE MORE AS ITS SPINNING AND ORBITING THE SUN.

THE CRUST OF THE EARTH SURROUNDS ITS MOLTEN IRON ALLOY INNER CORE, ONCE PLANET X BEGINS TO ORBT THE SUN (ABOUT 70 AU AWAY), THE CRUST OF THE EARTH WILL BEGIN TO SHIFT THE NORTH AND SOUTH POLES AS IT BREAKS FREE FROM ITS MOLTEN IRON ALLOY CORE. PLANET X ORBIT OF THE SUN WILL SHIFT THE EARTH'S CRUST WILL AND SET OFF THE RING OF FIRE, THE YELLOWSTONE VOLCANO --- AS WELL AS EARTHQUAKES, TSUNAMIS, HURRICANES, TORNADOES, FLOODS AND UNBRIDLED CIVIL CHAOS.

ONCE PLANET X BREAKS THROUGH BOTH THE OORT CLOUD ASTEROID BELT AND THEN THE KUIPER ASTEROID BELT, IT WILL SHOWER PLANET EARTH WITH LITERALLY HUNDREDS OF ASTEROIDS.

AN ASTEROID OF 10 METERS (32.8 FEET) WILL BURN OUT DUE TO EARTH'S ATMOSPHERE. AN ASTEROID 20 METERS TO 60 METERS (65.6 FEET TO 196.8 FEET) CAN WIPE OUT A CITY, AND AN ASTEROID THAT MEASURES 100 METERS TO 150 METERS (328 FEET TO 738 FEET) CAN WIPE OUT AN ENTIRE COUNTRY.
THE HUGE ASTEROID MEASURING 7.4 MILES (39,600 FEET) IN DIAMETER HIT THE YUCATAN PENINSULA ABOUT 66 MILLION YEARS AGO AND WIPED OUT THE DINOSAURS AND 3/4TH OF THE HUMAN POPULATION. SO IT IS IMPERATIVE THAT MANKIND FINDS A WAY TO NUDGE ASTEROIDS AWAY FROM EARTH AND/OR BEGIN TO REALIZE AND ACKNOWLEDGE THAT ALMIGHTY GOD IS IN TOTAL CONTROL OF PLANET X AND WILL BACKSLIDE IT OUTSIDE OUR SOLAR SYSTEM IF THE GLOBAL POPULATION BEGINS TO OBEY HIS COMMANDMENT OF PROPER MORAL LIVING.
WORTH REPEATING OVER AND OVER AGAIN IS, **"DON'T BE SCARED, JUST GET PREPARED"** BY REPENTING AND THEN ACCEPTING JESUS (YESHUA) AS YOUR LORD AND SAVIOR. IN DOING SO, IF AND WHEN PLANET X DOES DESTRUCTIVELY ORBIT OUR SUN, YOU WILL BE RAPTURE UP FROM THE EARTH UNTO HEAVEN. THOSE REMAINING ON EARTH WILL BE THE ONES WHO TURNED THEIR BACK ON THE GOOD LORD'S MERCY AND GRACE OF SALVATION. IT'S YOUR OWN CHOICE AS TO A HEAVENLY "LIGHT" OR A SATANIC **DARKNESS**.
RIGHT NOW THE SUN IS SHOOTING OUT TREMENDOUS SOLAR FLARES, THERE ARE MANY, MANY MORE ACTIVE VOLCANOES EARTHQUAKES, HURRICANES, TSUNAMIS, TORNADOES AND FLOODS --- ALONG WITH SHORTAGE OF WATER, FOOD AND OTHER NECESSITIES IN VARIOUS PARTS OF THE GLOBE.

BE WISE IN THE LORD AND YOU WILL BE SAVED.

THE SPIRITUALLY WISE SEE ALL THIS HAPPENING, AND THE CUNNING SCORN AND LAUGH AT ALL THE MANY PROPHETIC SIGNS AND WARNINGS..

AFFIRMATION OF PLANET X

IF AND WHEN PLANET X ORBITS OUR SUN, IT WILL SET OFF THE MANY VOLCANOES AND EARTHQUAKES LOCATED NEAR AND AROUND **THE RING OF FIRE**. AS THE PICTURE SHOWN BELOW DEPICTS THE GLOBAL NATURE OF **THE RING OF FIRE**.

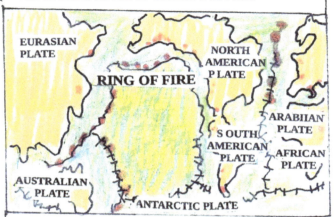

IT IS IMPORTANT TO KNOW THAT 75% OF ALL THE VOLCANOES AND 90% OF THE EARTHQUAKES ARE LOCATED IN THE RING OF FIRE. IT IS ALSO VERY IMPORTANT TO REALIZE THAT THE YELLOWSTONE AND OTHER VOLCANOES ARE PART OF THE EPIC VOLCANO AND EARTHQUAKE CENTER.

THE OUTER CRUST OF THE EARTH IS 18 MILES DEEP, BUT IT IS ONLY 3 MILES DEEP UNDER THE OCEAN. THE LOWER (UNDER THE OCEAN) CRUST IS MUCH MORE LIGHT AND BRITTLE AND CAN BREAK SENDING AN EARTHQUAKE AND A RAGING TSUNAMI HUNDREDS AND HUNDREDS OF MILES AWAY.

SUCH A SITUATION CAN EASILY WIPE OUT ABOUT 80 PERCENT OF THE EARTH'S POPULATION, AS THE HUGE TSUNAMI CAN FLOOD 100 TO 150 MILES ON THE INLAND COASTAL REGIONS AROUND THE GLOBE.

ADD TO THE ABOVE TRAGIC CATASTROPHIC TRAGEDY TO HUMAN LIFE ARE THE ASTEROIDS THAT WILL PLUMMET EARTH, THE HURRICANES, THE TORNADOES, THE BOLTS OF TREMENDOUS LIGHTNING, THE CIVIL DISOBEDIENCE OF PEOPLE KILLING EACH OTHER FOR FOOD. WATER AND OTHER IMMORAL THINGS.

AGAIN AND AGAIN, YOU MUST KNOW AND WELL REALIZE THAT YOU, **'DON'T BE SCARED, JUST GET PREPARED."**

RIGHT THIS MOMENT, WHEREVER YOU ARE, JUST REPENT OF YOUR SINS, ACCEPT JESUS (YESHUA) AS YOUR LORD AND SAVIOR AND ASK FOR HIS HOLY SPIRIT TO RAISE YOU UP BEFORE PLANET X ORBITS THE SUN.

HOW THE EARTH GENERATES THE ELECTROMAGNETIC FIELD

THE **OUTER CRUST** OF THE EARTH IS 18 MILES (30 KILOMETERS) THICK. THE **INNER CRUST** OF THE EARTH IS THREE MILES THICK AND IS LIGHT, BRITTLE AND EASILY PRONE TO BREAK.

THE **MANTEL** IS MORE FLEXIBLE. IT FLOWS INSTEAD OF FRACTURING AND EXTENDS 1,800 MILES (2,000 KILOMETERS) BELOW THE SURFACE.

THE **INNER MOLTEN CORE** IS 1,500 MILES THICK (2,400 KILOMETERS) AND MOVES TOWARD THE WEST.

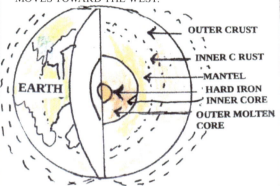

THE **INNER HARD IRON CORE** IS 1,500 MILES THICK (1,220 KILOMETERS) MOVES TOWARD THE EAST, AND IS ABOUT 70 PERCENT OF THE MOON'S RADIUS.
THE TEMPERATURE OF THE **HARD INNER CORE** IS ABOUT 10,000 F WHICH IS ABOUT THE TEMPERATURE OF THE SURFACE OF THE SUN.

THE **HARD INNER CORE** IS WHITE HOT BUT THE PRESSURE ON IT IS SO HIGH IT CANNOT MELT. BUT SOME SCIENTISTS THINK THE **HARD INNER CORE** IS MELTING SOME WHAT.

THE EASTWARD MOVEMENT OF THE **HARD INNER CORE** AND THE WESTWARD MOVEMENT OF THE **MOLTEN OUTER CORE** IS THE FRICTION THAT GENERATES THE EARTH'S ELECTROMAGNETIC FIELD. HOWEVER, SOME SCIENTISTS THINK THAT THE EARTH'S MAGNETIC FIELD IS WEAKENING DUE TO PLANET X NOW ENTERING OUT SOLAR SYSTEM. PLANET X MAY HAVE CAUSED THE EXTRA TILT OF THE EARTH AND CAUSED IT TO WOBBLE AND AFFECTS THE HARD INNER AND OUTER MOLTEN CORES TO SPIN ERACTICALLY.

THE SUN'S INNER CORE IS 27 MILLION DEGREES FAHRENHEIT. PLANET X INNER CORE COULD BE 2-5 MILLION DEGREES FAHRENHEIT.

AFFIRMATION OF PLANET X

THE MAGNETIC POLES OF THE SUN ACTUALLY FLIP EVERY 11 YEARS. THE MAGNETIC POLES OF THE SUN WEAKEN AND REDUCE TO ZERO, AND THEN EMERGE WITH OPPOSITE NORTH AND SOUTH POLE POLARITY --- WHICH IS A REGULAR 11 YEAR SOLAR CYCLE OF THE SUN. AND IS DUE ANY MOMENT.

THE TREMENDOUS POWER PRODUCING CAPABILITY OF THE SUN IS WITNESSED BY THE 27 MILLION DEGREE FAHRENHEIT TEMPERATURE OF ITS INNER CORE..

THE HUMAN ELECTROMAGNETIC PULSE (EMP) WEAPON CAN ALSO DESTROY A NATION'S ELECTRICAL GRID. IT WOULD WIPE OUT A NATION'S POWER TRANSFORMERS. THUS POWER COULD NOT BE TRANSMITTED MILES AWAY AND OR REDUCED FOR ELECTRICAL POWER FOR SAFETY IN THE HOME.

HOMELAND SECURITY IS IN THE PROCESS OF SETTING UP RECOVERY TRANSFORMERS FOR EMERGENCY PURPOSES, BUT ONLY EFFECTIVE IF ON E CAN DEPICT A SUDDEN (CME) UPON WHICH THEY CAN THEN SHUT DOWN THE ELECTRICAL POWER GRID ON EARTH.

IF AN UNEXPECTED (EMC) HITS, THE RESULT WOULD NOT BE ENOUGH POWER WATER, FOOD, MEDICINE, AND OTHER NEEDS.

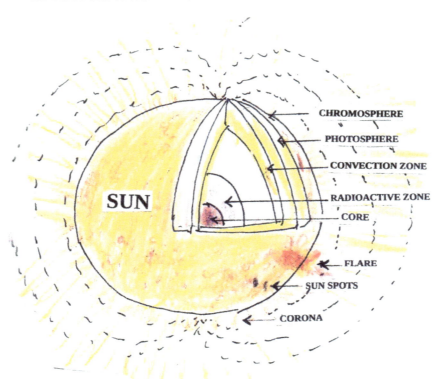

IF PLANET X DOES ORBIT OUR SUN, AND SETS OFF THE **RING OF FIRE**, THE SMOKE AND FIRE FROM THE VOLCANIC ERUPTIONS, IT WILL BLOCK THE SUN'S LIGHT, AND WE WILL NOT HAVE GLOBAL WARMING, WE WILL HAVE A GLOBAL ICE AGE ACROSS THE GLOBE.

PLANET EARTH'S INNER CORE HAS A 10,700 FAHRENHEIT AND ITS MAGNETIC FIELD HAS BEEN WEAKENING ... WHICH IS DESIGNED TO REFLECT THE SUN'S SPORADIC, HUGE SOLAR FLARES. THIS GIVE YOU A PERSPECTIVE OF WHAT CAN OCCUR IF PLANET X (WHICH IS A MINIATURE SOLAR SYSTEM WITH SEVEN PLANETS AND VARIOUS MOONS) WERE TO ORBIT OUR SUN. SUCH A SITUATION WOULD COMPLETELY DESTROY THE EARTH AND TOTALLY DISRUPT ALL THE OTHER PLANETS. A GEOMAGNETIC STORM TRIGGERED BY A BURST OF THE SUN'S SOLAR ENERGY CALLED A CORONAL MASS EJECTION (CME) COULD WIPE OUT THE TOTAL GLOBAL ELECTRICAL AND ELECTRONIC POWER GRID.

THE WORST SUN'S (CME) FLARED EARTH IN 1859 IN WHICH THE SUN'S RAYS ELECTRICALLY SHOCKED THE TELEGRAPH OPERATORS AND SET FIRE TO THE TELEGRAPH PAPER.

AFFIRMATION OF PLANET X

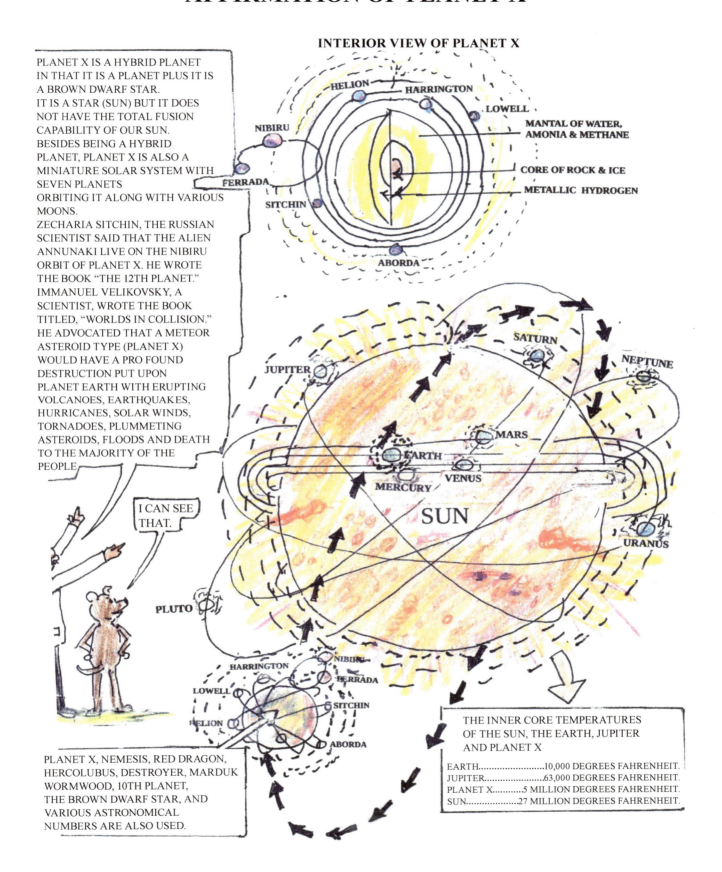

AFFIRMATION OF PLANET X

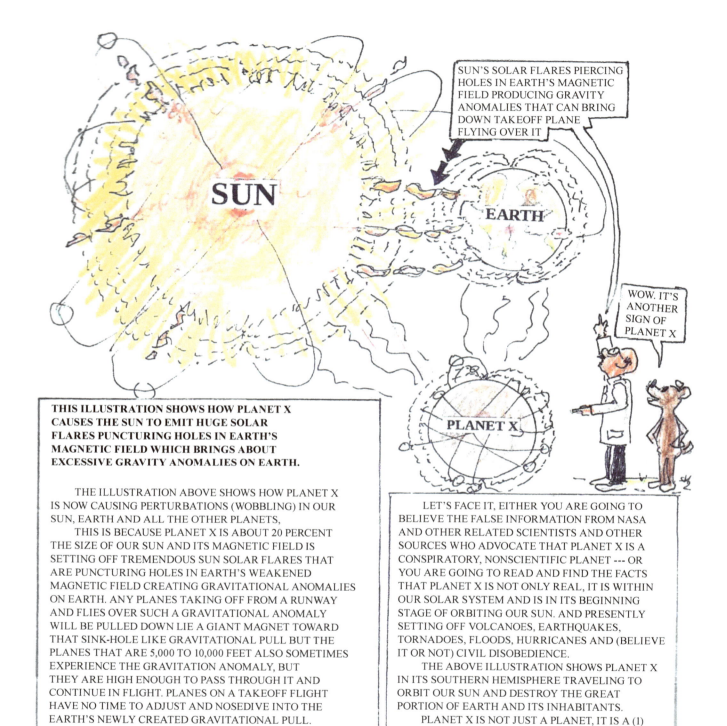

THIS ILLUSTRATION SHOWS HOW PLANET X CAUSES THE SUN TO EMIT HUGE SOLAR FLARES PUNCTURING HOLES IN EARTH'S MAGNETIC FIELD WHICH BRINGS ABOUT EXCESSIVE GRAVITY ANOMALIES ON EARTH.

THE ILLUSTRATION ABOVE SHOWS HOW PLANET X IS NOW CAUSING PERTURBATIONS (WOBBLING) IN OUR SUN, EARTH AND ALL THE OTHER PLANETS,

THIS IS BECAUSE PLANET X IS ABOUT 20 PERCENT THE SIZE OF OUR SUN AND ITS MAGNETIC FIELD IS SETTING OFF TREMENDOUS SUN SOLAR FLARES THAT ARE PUNCTURING HOLES IN EARTH'S WEAKENED MAGNETIC FIELD CREATING GRAVITATIONAL ANOMALIES ON EARTH. ANY PLANES TAKING OFF FROM A RUNWAY AND FLIES OVER SUCH A GRAVITATIONAL ANOMALY WILL BE PULLED DOWN LIE A GIANT MAGNET TOWARD THAT SINK-HOLE LIKE GRAVITATIONAL PULL BUT THE PLANES THAT ARE 5,000 TO 10,000 FEET ALSO SOMETIMES EXPERIENCE THE GRAVITATION ANOMALY, BUT THEY ARE HIGH ENOUGH TO PASS THROUGH IT AND CONTINUE IN FLIGHT. PLANES ON A TAKEOFF FLIGHT HAVE NO TIME TO ADJUST AND NOSEDIVE INTO THE EARTH'S NEWLY CREATED GRAVITATIONAL PULL.

SOME AIRPORTS ARE NOW CLOSED DUE TO SUCH GRAVITATIONAL ANOMALIES. LARGER AIRPORTS CAN ADJUST AND NOT USE RUNWAYS AREAS WHERE THE GRAVITY IS OVERLY STRONG.

LET'S FACE IT, EITHER YOU ARE GOING TO BELIEVE THE FALSE INFORMATION FROM NASA AND OTHER RELATED SCIENTISTS AND OTHER SOURCES WHO ADVOCATE THAT PLANET X IS A CONSPIRATORY, NONSCIENTIFIC PLANET --- OR YOU ARE GOING TO READ AND FIND THE FACTS THAT PLANET X IS NOT ONLY REAL, IT IS WITHIN OUR SOLAR SYSTEM AND IS IN ITS BEGINNING STAGE OF ORBITING OUR SUN. AND PRESENTLY SETTING OFF VOLCANOES, EARTHQUAKES, TORNADOES, FLOODS, HURRICANES AND (BELIEVE IT OR NOT) CIVIL DISOBEDIENCE.

THE ABOVE ILLUSTRATION SHOWS PLANET X IN ITS SOUTHERN HEMISPHERE TRAVELING TO ORBIT OUR SUN AND DESTROY THE GREAT PORTION OF EARTH AND ITS INHABITANTS.

PLANET X IS NOT JUST A PLANET, IT IS A (1) HYBRID PLANET LIKE STAR, (2) A SECOND SUN IN OUR SOLAR SYSTEM, AND (3) A MINIATURE SOLAR SYSTEM WITH SEVEN SMALL PLANETS AND MOONS ORBITING IT.

NOTE; THIS EXAMPLE IS NOT TO SCALE. IT IS ONLY FOR ILLUSTRATION PURPOSES.

AFFIRMATION OF PLANET X

Is it possible that "Planet X" caused the crashes of the
2019 Ehtiopian 767 and the 2018 Lion Boeing 737 crashes

How so?

Diagram A shows the take off from the runway of both the 2018 Lion Boeing 737 plane and the 2019 Ethiopian Boeing 767 plane. Notice that both were in their "take off" mode. So, either both Boeing planes had an electronic or pilot error ... or some other ground/space anomaly occurred.

According to a Planet X Physicists, Claudia Albers, the entrance of Planet X into our Solar System has affected the Sun's magnetic field and resultantly tremendous solar flares are now firing out from the Sun towards Planet Earth.

It is no secret that Planet Earth is now beyond its normal 23.5 degree tilt and its magnetic field has definitely weakened. Thus, the extremely high solar flares from the Sun has punctured wholes in the Earth's magnetic field. Wherever those solar flare holes are in Earth's magnetic field, it releases an extremely high gravitational pull in that punctured space on Earth.

Upon takeoff, if a Boeing plane hovers over that intense gravitational space, it will pull the plane down like a gravitational sink hole. There is little or no time to accelerate as the weight of the plane falls victim to the Earth's uncommon gravitational pull of that particular area. Some airports have been closed because of such high gravity pulls.

This diagram A (below) shows how the take offs of the 2018 Lion Boeing 737 take off from the runway, as well as the 2019 Ethiopian Boeing 767 take off had little of no time for pilot reaction when the intense gravitational pull crash dragged their planes into the Earth.

Diagram B is a different story all together. This is where a Boeing 737 or 767 is flying at an altitude between 5,000 to 10,000 feet. Noticed that they too can hit AIR POCKETS and/or the infamous GRAVITATIONAL ANOMALY, however, the pilot has the time and extra speed to pull through the sudden drop and continue the planes upward flight pattern.

THE AIRLINE PILOTS ARE NOW NOTIFYING THE TRAFFIC
CONTROLLERS WHERE AND WHEN THEY
FLY INTO ANY AIR POCKETS OR
ESPECIALLY GRAVITATIONAL
ANOMALIES.

AFFIRMATION OF PLANET X

FACING THE PEOPLE AND FACTS ABOUT PLANET X

THE ANTARCTIC

THE 2017 ANTARCTICA ICEBERG BREAK (THE SIZE OF DELAWARE) MAKES THE **GULF STREAM LESS SALINE**, IN WHICH THE COLD WATER FROM THE ICEBERG PUSHES THE WARM SALT WATER DEEP INTO THE OCEAN.

BY THIS COLD WATER OVERTAKING THE WARM SALT WATER, THE U. S. NEW ENGLAND AND THE COUNTRY OF ENGLAND WILL HAVE A MUCH COLDER WINTER WEATHER.

ALL THIS WILL CHANGE THE WEATHER PATTERN --- AS WELL AS THE JET STREAM CAUSING FARMERS TO WONDER WHAT IS THE BEST TIME TO PLANT THEIR CROPS.

THE ANTARCTIC AND THE ARCTIC ICE MAKE UP COMPRISE 90% OF ALL OF EARTH'S ICE. IF THE ANTARCTICA WERE TO MELT ENTIRELY, THE SEAL LEVEL WOULD RISE 190 FEET.

WORD HAS IT THAT THE WARMING OF THE ANTARCTICA IS CAUSED BY THE ENTRANCE OF PLANET X IN OUR SOLAR SYSTEM.

IF THIS BE TRUE, THEN INSTEAD OF BEING CONCERNED ABOUT GLOBAL WARMING, THE END RESULT WILL VERY WELL BE AN ICE AGE ... AS IF AND WHEN PLANET X BREAKS THROUGH THE KUIPER ASTEROID BELT, AND BEGINS TO ORBIT OUR SUN, THEN IT WILL SET OFF THE **RING OF FIRE** AND THE OVERLAPPING OF THE TEUTONIC PLATES WILL SET OFF THE MULTITUDE OF VOLCANOES AND EARTHQUAKES IN WHICH THE SMOKE AND FIRE WILL BLACKEN THE SUN LEADING TO AN ICE AGE.

BUT "**DON'T BE SCARED, JUST GET PREPARED**," BY REPENTING AND ACCEPTING JESUS (YESHUA) AS YOUR LORD AND SAVIOR AND ASKING FOR HIS HOLY SPIRIT TO RAPTURE YOU UP ... IF AND WHEN PLANET X ORBITS OUR SUN.

THE ARCTIC CIRCLE

ACCORDING TO SCIENTIFIC REPORTS THE ARCTIC AND THE ANTARCTICA ARE LOSING ICE MASS SINCE 2002.

SEA ICE REFLECTS THE SUN MUCH MORE EFFICIENTLY THAN THE OCEAN WATER. SEA ICE REFLECTS ABOUT 70 PERCENT OF THE SUNS RAYS BACK INTO SPACE.

THE ICE MASS IN THE ARCTIC CIRCLE COVERS ABOUT 30 TO 40 PERCENT LESS THAN IT DID IN THE 1970'S.

MELTED ICE PROVIDES THE SAFE DRINKING WATER FOR THE PEOPLE AROUND THE GLOBE,

FROZEN ICE IN THE ARCTIC AND THE ANTARCTICA CAN EXTEND TO ABOUT 200 FEET BELOW THE SURFACE.

THE ANTARCTIC IS COLDER AS IT HAS MOUNTAINS 900 FEET ABOVE THE OCEAN WHILE THE ARCTIC IS ABOUT ONE FOOT ABOVE ITS OCEAN.

PLANET X IS AFFECTING BOTH THE ARCTIC AND ANTARCTIC ATMOSPHERES AND MELTING THE ICE AT A RECORD SPEED WHICH THEN EMITS MORE CO2 (CARBOON DIOXIDE) IN THE AIR CAUSING EXCESSIVE WARMING.

THE "CARBON BOMB" ARE THE ARCTIC ICE BUGS WHICH ONCE THE ICE MELTS, THE ICE BUGS BELCH OUT THE GREEN-HOUSE GASES OF CARBON DIOXIDE AND METHANE FURTHER BRINGING ABOUT GLOBAL WARMING.

THE REAL END RESULT IS AN "ICE AGE" WHENEVER PLANET X ACTUALLY ORBITS THE SUN AND SETS OF THE **RING OF FIRE VOLCANIC ERUPTION** WHOSE SMOKE AND FIRE WILL BLACKEN THE SUN LEADING TO FEARCE COLD WINTERY WINDS AND ICE.

AFFIRMATION OF PLANET X

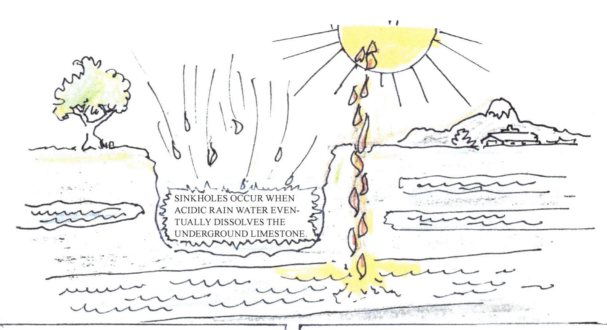

ACCORDING TO VARIOUS DEPARTMENT OF ENVIRONMENTAL PROTECTION AGENCIES THE ACIDIC RAIN WATER DISSOLVES THE LIME STONE RESULTING IN A SINKHOLE.

SINKHOLES CAN ALSO BE CAUSED BY PUMPING UNDERGROUND WATER FOR AGRICULTURE, INDUSTRIAL USES AND EVEN FOR DRINKING PURPOSES.

OTHER CAUSES OF SINKHOLES ARE EXCESSIVE BUILDING OF HOMES, HUGE PARKING LOTS FOR DEPARTMENT STORES ALL OF WHICH PROVIDES A SLOUGH OF RUSHING WATER BUILDING UP IN A LOWER LEVEL OF THE GROUND. EVENTUALLY THE ACIDIC WATER PERCOLATES THROUGH THE LIMESTONE RESULTING IN A COLLAPSED SINKHOLE.

SINKHOLES ARE FOUND IN PRACTICALLY EVERY STATE AS WELL AS AROUND THE WORLD. SINKHOLES HAVE FOUND THEIR WAY ALONG THE SHORES OF THE DEAD SEA, AND ALSO RECENTLY IN NEW ZEALAND.

ANOTHER POTENTIAL CAUSE OF SINKHOLES IS THE POSSIBILITY OF PLANET X CAUSING THE SUN TO SHED TREMENDOUS SOLAR FLARES TO PLUMMET INTO THE EARTH'S SURFACE AND DRYING UP THE UNDERGROUND WATER WAYS.

THE CHEMTRAILS ARE ANOTHER CAUSE OF THE SINKHOLES, AS THE CHEMICALS OF BARIUM ALUMINUM, MAGNESIUM AND OTHER CHEMICALS CAN CAUSE TERRIFIC RAIN STORMS. BASICALLY IT IS THE HEAVY WEIGHT OF THE BARIUM IN THE CLOUDS THAT BURST INTO TORRENTIAL DOWNFALL OF ACIDIC RAIN WHICH ITS WEIGHT OVERLOADS THE CLOUDS.

SO, THE COMBINATION OF (1) POROUS LIMESTONE, (2) HEAVY RAIN FROM THE BARIUM IN THE CHEMTRAILS, (3) THE OVER BUILDING OF HOMES, FACTORIES, AND OTHER MASS CONSTRUCTION, (4) PUMPING OUT THE UNDERGROUND WATER FOR AGRICULTURE, INDUSTRIAL USES, AND DRINKING, AND (5) PLANET X AFFECTING THE SUN TO SHOOT OUT TREMENDOUS SOLAR FLARES PENETRATING INTO THE EARTH'S UNDERGROUND WATER WAYS,

SETTING UP DESALINATION PLANTS NEAR OCEAN AND LAKES CAN OFFSET MUCH OF THE SINKHOLES SITUATIONS ... PROVIDING GOVERNMENT RESTRICTIONS ARE UPDATED TO MEET CURRENT POPULATION AND ENVIRONMENTAL NEEDS.

AMOS 5:24 LET JUSTICE ROLL ON LIKE A RIVER, RIGHTEOUSNESS LIKE A NEVER-FAILING STREAM.

REMEMBER, **DON'T BE SCARED, JUST GET PREPARED**. THE LORD IS RETURNING SOON.

SO TRUE. AMEN.

AFFIRMATION OF PLANET X

DON'T BE SCARED, JUST GET PREPARED.

NOW THAT WE KNOW PLANET X IS NOT JUST A PLANET, IT IS ACTUALLY A HYBRID TYPE PLANET IN THAT IT IS (1) A SUN LIKE STAR, BUT IT DOES NOT HAVE THE FUSION CAPABILITY OF THE SUN; (2) IT HAS SEVEN PLANETS AND A FEW MOONS ORBITING IT; AND IT DEFINITELY IS A MINIATURE SOLAR SYSTEMS NOW EXISTING INSIDE OUR LARGER SOLAR SYSTEM.

SUCH A MINIATURE SOLAR SYSTEM HAS A TREMENDOUS EFFECT ON ALL OF THE MAJOR AND MINOR PLANETS THAT DEFINITELY INCLUDES PLANET EARTH.

PLANET X EVEN HAS AN EFFECT ON THE SUN IN THAT IT IS CAUSING HUGE SOLAR FLARES BREAKING THROUGH PLANET EARTH'S MAGNETIC FIELD WHICH ARE IGNITING EARTHQUAKES, VOLCANOES, TORNADOES, FLOODS, HURRICANES AS WELL AS CIVIL UNREST AND HUMAN CANCER AND OTHER IMMUNE AND BRAIN DISORDERS.

THE PLANET X PHYSICISTS, CLAUDIA ALBERS EQUATES THIS HYBRID TYPE PLANET TO BE IN DIRECT PROPORTION TO THE DISTINCTION OF UNRIGHTEOUS ANCIENT CIVILIZATIONS.

SOME SCIENTISTS CALL PLANET X THE "SECOND EVIL SUN," WHILE THE THEOLOGICAL TYPE SCIENTISTS LIKE DR. CLAUDIA ALBERS IS INCLINED TO CALL PLANET X "THE JUDGMENT STAR" THAT IS SENT DESTRUCTIVELY FORTH BY THE LORD GOD WHENEVER MANKIND HAS CLEARLY TURNED THEIR BACK ON GOD'S COMMANDMENTS.

PLANET X IS CAUSING THE SUN'S SOLAR FLARES TO PENETRATE EARTH'S MAGNETIC FIELD SETTING UP GRAVITATIONAL ANOMALIES WHEREBY A PLANE TAKING OFF THE RUNWAY IS PULLED DOWN INTO A CRASH LANDING BY THE NEWLY STRONG GRAVITY.

SATAN IS BEHIND ALL THIS TAKING PLACE IN NOT ONLY IN THE SOLAR SYSTEM, BUT ALSO IN TAKING OVER THE MINDS OF MANY UNRIGHTEOUS HUMANS. BUT WORRY NOT FOR ALMIGHTY GOD AND HIS ONLY BEGOTTEN SON, JESUS CHRIST (YESHUA) HAS SET THE STAGE FOR ALL THIS TO HAPPEN EXACTLY ACCORDING TO HIS DECIDING TIME, PLACE AND EVENTS.

SO ... "**DON'T BE SCARED, JUST GET PREPARED.**" THIS IS DONE BY (1) TRULY REPENTING OF YOUR SINS. REMEMBER, THOUGH, REPENTANCE IS NOT JUST JUST SAYING YOUR ARE SORRY, IT INVOLVES A COMPLETE CHANGE IN YOUR LIFESTYLE. (2) THEN ACCEPTING JESUS (YESHUA) AS YOUR TRUE LORD AND SAVIOR; (3) AND THEN ASKING FOR THE HOLY SPIRIT (WHO RAISED JESUS FROM THE DEAD) TO ALSO RAPTURE YOU UP ---IF AND WHEN PLANET X APOCALYPTIC ORBIT OF OUR SUN TAKES PLACE.

THE GOVERNMENT, THE MILITARY, THE VATICAN, THE FREEMASONS, THE ILLUMINATI, THE FEDERAL RESERVE AS WELL AS MANY ESOTERIC PEOPLES HAVE UNDERGROUND BUNKERS IN WHICH TO HIDE.

HOWEVER, THEY WILL NOT HAVE THE SECURITY AND SAFE SALVATION OF THOSE WHO TRUST IN THE LORD GOD'S WORDS.

PLEASE DO KEEP IN MIND THAT THOSE WHO **ROB, MURDER, STEAL, GOSSIP, DRUNKEN, DRUG RELATED, IMMORAL SEX, MURDER AND OBEY** NOT THE LAW WILL NOT BE RAPTURE UP.

YOU CANNOT FOOL THE LORD GOD WITH FALSE INTENTIONS.

HERE IS AN OUTLINE OF WHAT YOU READ SO FAR.

TOPIC   EXPLANATION   PAGE

(1) AFFIRMATION OF PLANET X BY ROBERT S HARRINGTON:
Robert S Harrington flew to Iceland to confirmed the existence of Planet X along with its exact coordinates. He was the Head of the Naval Observatory in Washington, DC. Not long after he observed Planet X, he died suddenly.. 61

(2) AFFIRMATION OF PLANET X BY JESUIT PRIESTS MALACHI MARTIN:
Malachi Martin had a few Doctorate Degrees and had access to the Catholic Infrared Telescope in Arizona that is handled by the Jesuit Order of Priests. The Jesuit Priests are some of the most intelligent people on Earth. However Malachi Martin left the Jesuit Order as he thought they had become too secular, and were being falsely and convincingly led by Satanic Humanoids............. 62

(3) AFFIRMATION OF PLANET X VIA TELESCOPIC AND CHEMTRAIL COVER UP: Since Planet X is now inside our Solar System, it is affecting the Magnetic Field of our Sun. The metal core of our Sun is 27 million degrees Fahrenheit and the liquid core surrounding it 12 degrees Fahrenheit. The metal core turns one way and the liquid core turns in the opposite direction thus friction is caused and establishes the Sun's Magnetic Field. The problem now, it that Planet X Magnetic Field is making the Sun's Magnetic Field touch one another thus sending out tremendous Sun Solar Flares upon Earth. They (?) (I know who) are paying pilots to fly planes to spread dangerous and toxic chemicals across globe try and block the Sun's Solar Flares. Do not confuse Contrails that came out of a plane's engine with Chemtrails that come out of a plane's pipes located on the wings of the plane. The chemtrails murder people 63

(4) AFFIRMATION OF PLANET X IS SUN'S SOLAR FLARES
The Sun is shooting off more Solar Flares than ever before. Once Planet X travels through the (1) Oort Cloud of Icy Comets, (2) The Kuoiper Belt of Meteorites and the (3) Asteroid Belt of Asteroids ... Planet X will then orbit our Sun causing the Tectonic Plates to shift hundreds and even thousands of miles apart. That will make the thousands of volcanoes on Earth explode whose smoke and fire will make the Sun turn black, the Moon to lose its light, and the asteroids between Mars and Jupiter will apocalyptically destroy Planet Earth. 64, 65

(5) At the End Time the asteroids between Mars and Jupiter will **CATASTROPHICALLY PLUMMET THE EARTH.**
If Planet X does eventually orbit our Sun, it will cause the Tectonic Plates to ship hundreds and even thousands iof miles apart and cause the asteroids between Mars and Jupiter to catastrophically plummet the Earth 65

(73)

(6) AFFIRMATION OF PLANET X BY POTENTIAL RING OF FIRE.
It is well known that 90% of earthquakes and 75% of the volcanoes are around the Ring of Fire The outer crust of the Earth is 18 miles deep, but is only 3 miles deep under the ocean. If the Ring of Fire Volcanoes fire off it will easily easily wipe at 80% of the people on Earth. Moreover, there will be tremendous hurricanes, tornadoes and colossal bolts of lighting and flood like rain. But don't be scared. Just get "Born Again" prepared. By accepting Jesus as your Lord and Savior, turning 180degrees from sin, and asking for Father God's Holy Spirit to RAPTURE you BEFORE THE "END TIME" TRIBULATION 66

(7) AFFIRMATION OF PLANET X COULD WIPE OUT EARTH'S ELECTRICAL POWER GRID.
A Geomagnetic Storm triggered by the Sun's burst called a Coronal Global Mass Ejection ((CME) could wipe out total Global Electrical and Electronic Power Grids. One (CME) occurred in 1859. If Planeet X does orbit our Sun, and the smoke and fire blackens the Sun, the Earth will have an ICE AGE. Again, don't be scared. Just get "BORN AGAIN" prepared 67

(8) AFFIRMATION OF PLANET X IS A MINIATURE SOLAR SYSTEM WITH SEVERAL PLANETS AND MOONS ORBITING IT.
Planet X sits outside our Solar System, but Almighty God sends it inside our Solar System whenever Humankind falls below the unrighteousness of Sodom & Gomorrah. Once inside our Solar System, Planet X disrupts the Sun's Magnetic Field as well as Earth's Magnetic Field. This, then, causes the Sun to shoot off Solar Flares in which many cause a great deal of destruction on Earth. Some of the other names of Planet X are The Brown Dwarf Star, Red Dragon, Hercolubus, Marduk, Wormwood, 18th Planet, as well as other names 68

(9) AFFIRMATION OF PLANET X IS CAUSING WOBBLING PERTURBATIONS OF PLANET EARTH.
Some scientists estimate that Planet X is about 20% the size of the Sun. As a warning to the global Community, Planet X has three different speech and a very hard to detect. It does, however, cause floods, volcano eruptions, hurricanes, as well as (believe it or not) causes civil disobedience 69

(10) AFFIRMATION OF PLANET X IN AIRPORTS, ANTARCTIC, SINKHOLES, AND HUMAN HEALTH PROBLEMS.
(1) Planet X causes the Sun to shoot off solar flares unto Airport Runways causing planes to crash. (2) It is also causing gigantic Icebergs to break free from the Antarctic making significant weather patterns changes as it travels up the Atlantic Ocean. (3) The Chemicals being sprayed by the Chemtrail Planets are causing torrential rain storms that make sinkholes. (4) ONCE AGAIN. DON'T BE SCARED. JUST GET PREPARED BY BEING "BORN AGAIN." 70, 71, 72

Ancient History of The Brown Dwarf Star and Planet X

The term "Nibiru" comes from the Sumerian Cuneiform Stone Tablets that are dated 6,000 years ago. The term Nibiru means "Planet of the crossing."

The Sumerian culture is the first recorded civilization on earth which is now called modern day Iraq ... including Mesopotamia and Babylon. The Sumerians were the first civilization to invent writing, math, science, medicine, astronomy and other fields of learning.

The Sumerian writings describe a Planets X that elliptically orbits the sun evry 3,600 years (contrary to the 2,160 years orbit) claimed by many other modern-day astronomers.

The Sumerians also claim (as was earlier published by Zechariah Sitchin) that they were visited by an alien race called the Annunaki which means "Princely Offspring."

Zechariah Sitchin wrote (in 1976) the book titled, "The 12th Planet." In that book, Sitchin expounds that the alien race called Anunnaki visited Earth when Planet X made its 3,600 year orbit. Astronomers and scientists describe Sitchin's book and thesis as --- pseudoscientific and preposterous. Nevertheless, Zachariah Sitchin sold 20 million copies of his book.

But that's up to you to accept, reject or modify Sitchin and Astronomer judgment as being --- scientific, religious, fact or just plain outright fiction.

However, there is no denying that 6,000 years ago, the Sumerians in Iraq made a Stone Tablet featuring the present day planets INCLUDING NIBIRU --- NOW CALLED THE BROWN DWARF STAR (OR PLANET X) ON THEIR STONE TABLET.

SHOWN HERE IS THE 6,000 YEAR OLD SUMERIAN STONE TABLET.

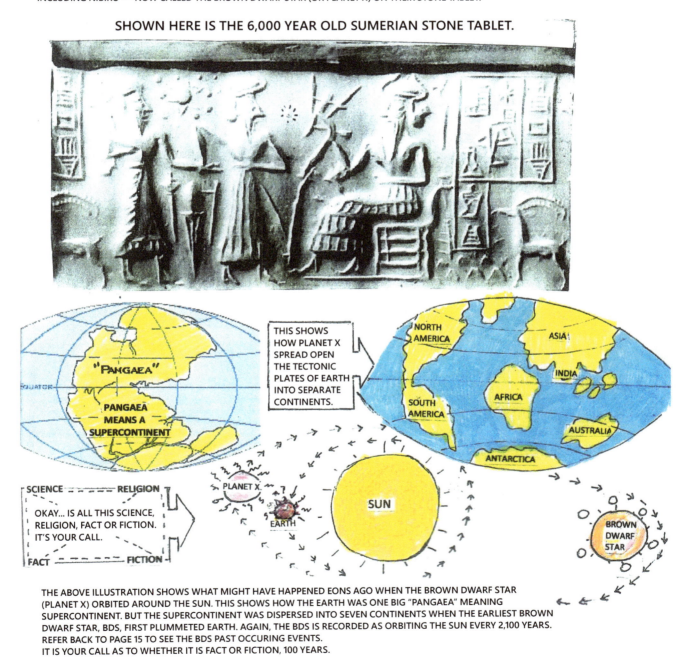

THE ABOVE ILLUSTRATION SHOWS WHAT MIGHT HAVE HAPPENED EONS AGO WHEN THE BROWN DWARF STAR (PLANET X) ORBITED AROUND THE SUN. THIS SHOWS HOW THE EARTH WAS ONE BIG "PANGAEA" MEANING SUPERCONTINENT. BUT THE SUPERCONTINENT WAS DISPERSED INTO SEVEN CONTINENTS WHEN THE EARLIEST BROWN DWARF STAR, BDS, FIRST PLUMMETED EARTH. AGAIN, THE BDS IS RECORDED AS ORBITING THE SUN EVERY 2,100 YEARS. REFER BACK TO PAGE 15 TO SEE THE BDS PAST OCCURING EVENTS.

IT IS YOUR CALL AS TO WHETHER IT IS FACT OR FICTION, 100 YEARS.

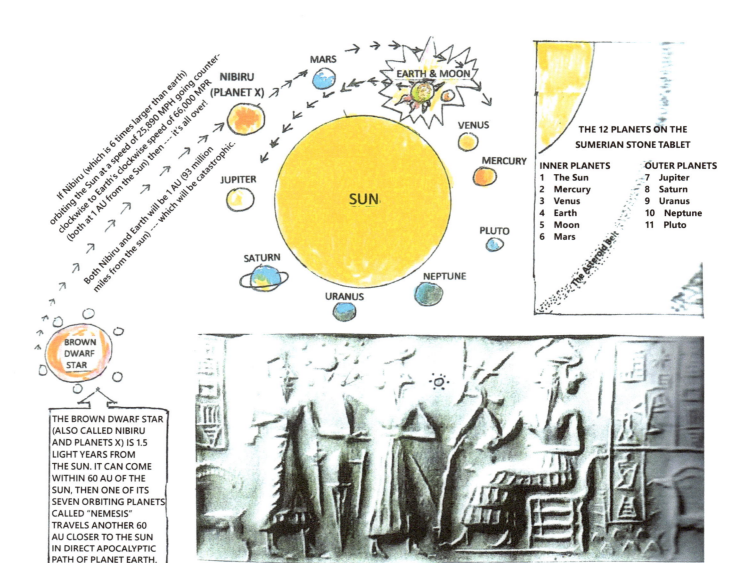

If Nibiru (which is 6 times larger than earth) orbiting the Sun at a speed of 25,890 MPH going counter-clockwise to Earth's clockwise speed of 66,000 MPH (both at 1 AU from the Sun) then --- it's all over! Both Nibiru and Earth will be 1 AU (93 million miles from the sun) --- which will be catastrophic.

THE 12 PLANETS ON THE SUMERIAN STONE TABLET

INNER PLANETS	OUTER PLANETS
1 The Sun	7 Jupiter
2 Mercury	8 Saturn
3 Venus	9 Uranus
4 Earth	10 Neptune
5 Moon	11 Pluto
6 Mars	

THE BROWN DWARF STAR (ALSO CALLED NIBIRU AND PLANETS X) IS 1.5 LIGHT YEARS FROM THE SUN. IT CAN COME WITHIN 60 AU OF THE SUN, THEN ONE OF ITS SEVEN ORBITING PLANETS CALLED "NEMESIS" TRAVELS ANOTHER 60 AU CLOSER TO THE SUN IN DIRECT APOCALYPTIC PATH OF PLANET EARTH.

REMEMBER, SOME OF THE SCIENTISTS SAY THE ENTIRE BROWN DWARF STAR ORBITS THE SUN.

AND SOME SAY THE BD STAR DOES NOT EVEN EXIST.

The chart shown above shows the alignment of the 12 planets (in which the Sumerians include the Sun as one of the 12 planets). This is according to the Sumerian Stone Tablet featured above. Not shown (in the Sumerian stone Tablet) is the Brown Dwarf Star (also called Nibiru, and Planet X) from which one of its seven orbiting planets travels apolitically close to Planet Earth.

The Sumerians claimed that the alien race called Anunnaki came from the 12th planet (Nibiru). Allegedly the Anunnaki landed on Planet Earth when the Nibiru Planet orbited close to it.

The number 12 proved to be the root of many sources of information from the Sumerian culture --- that we use today --- such as (12 inches in a foot), (12 eggs in a dozen), (12 hours in a day/night), the 12 tribes of Israel), (12 disciples of Jesus), (12 signs in the Zodiac), (12 Greek Olympians), (12 planets in our Solar System) ... and other such numerical signs.

Pluto was only discovered in 1930. It orbits the Sun every 248 years and is located about 2.67 billion miles from the Sun. The Brown Dwarf Star (which is about 40% the size of our Sun) is located approximately 1.5 light years from the Sun and was recorded 6,000 years ago by the Sumerians --- and as early as 1982 by American astronomers. It appears that the Brown Dwarf is within the gravitational pull of the Sun.

The Brown Dwarf Star comes within in 60 AU of the Sun, but one of its 7 orbiting planets (named Nemesis) travels another 60 Au toward the Sun putting it smack dab in a catastrophic line with Planet Earth. Question is --- does it orbit the sun every 2,160 years or 3,600 years.

The New York Times in June 19, 1982 reported that something out there in our Solar System is tugging at Uranus and Neptune perturbing the two giant planets irregularly in their orbiting pattern around the Sun.

THEORETICAL CONCLUSION: Possibly when Noah's flood overwhelmed the earth, the demons (who had cohabited with the human population) dispersed to Planet Nibiru along with some of their human hybrids.

We know the Angels and Archangels home is in heaven. As for the demons (Nibiru might be their resting home).

World Wide Return of The Jews to Israel

IN **ISAIAH 43:5-6** THE PROPHET ISAIAH SAID THE PEOPLE OF ISRAEL WILL RETURN TO THEIR HOMELAND FROM THE EAST, FROM THE WEST, FROM THE NORTH AND FROM THE SOUTH.

FROM THE EAST, SINCE ISRAEL'S INDEPENDENCE AS A COUNTRY WAS ACHIEVED IN 1948, THOUSANDS OF JEWS HAVE RETURNED TO THEIR HOMELAND FROM SURROUNDING ARAB COUNTRIES.

FROM THE WEST, DURING THE 1990'S, HUNDREDS OF THOUSANDS OF JEWS FLED FROM THE WEST --- INCLUDING WESTERN EUROPE, THE UNITED STATES AND ESPECIALLY FROM THE HOLOCAUST IN GERMANY.

FROM THE NORTH, MANY HUNDREDS OF THOUSANDS OF JEWS LIVING IN THE SOVIET UNION MOVED TO ISRAEL FROM RUSSIA AFTER GREAT PRESSURE OF OTHER NATIONS (AS WAS PROPHESIED BY ISAIAH).

FROM THE SOUTH, A MASSIVE MIGRATION OF JEWS CAME TO ISRAEL FROM ETHIOPIA ONLY AFTER AN ISRAEL ETHIOPIAN FUND PAID A RANSOM TO ETHIOPIA (AS WAS AGAIN PROPHESIED BY ISAIAH).

AS THE PROPHET **JEREMIAH 8:7-8** SAID, "I WILL SAVE MY PEOPLE FROM THE COUNTRIES OF THE WORLD. AND TODAY, WE SEE WITH OUR OWN EYES THE MASSIVE RETURN OF THE JEWS TO THEIR HOMELAND ... AND NOW. HAVE JERUSALEM AS THEIR CAPITAL.

IT IS WISE NOT TO JUDGE THE JEWS TOO HARSHLY AS DID BALAAM IN THE OLD TESTAMENT, FOR BALAAM ONLY SAW THE IMMORALITY OF THE ISRAELITES, AND THEN CONCLUDED THAT HE COULD CURSE THEM. HOWEVER, THE LORD GOD TOLD BALAAM TO BLESS THE ISRAELITES AND NOT TO CURSE THEM, FOR HE, ALONE, IS THE JUSTIFIER OF HIS CHOSEN PEOPLE. WE CANNOT PUNISH ANOTHER FAMILY'S CHILDREN, AND SO IT IS WITH GOD'S CHILDREN. HE, ALONE, BLESSES OF CURSES THE JEWS IN RELATION TO THEIR LIVING OR NOT LIVING HIS WORD ... AS THE LORD GOD DOES WITH ALL THE PEOPLES OF THE WORLD.

IT IS IMPERATIVE THAT THE GENTILES AS WELL AS THE JEWS READ AND KNOW BOTH THE OLD AND NEW TESTAMENT. UNDER THE **OLD TESTAMENT**, THE ISRAELITES JUDGED EACH OTHER UNDER THE "LAW."

UNDER THE **NEW TESTAMENT**, THE JEWS AS WELL AS THE GENTILES ARE JUDGED UNDER THE LORD JESUS (YESHUA) **MERCY** (UNDESERVED FORGIVENESS) AND HIS **GRACE** (UNMERITED FAVOR).

UNDER THE JESUS' UMBRELLA OF MERCY AND GRACE, WE NO LONGER NEED TO SACRIFICE ANIMALS TO ABSOLVE OUR SINS, FOR THE SHED BLOOD AND SUFFERING OF JESUS ON THE CROSS AT CALVARY NEED ONLY A ONE TIME SACRIFICE FOR ALL ETERNITY. NO LONGER IS THERE A NEED OF ANNUAL ANIMAL SACRIFICES.

TO GET A BETTER UNDERSTANDING OF HOW AND WHY JESUS (YESHUA) IS THE MESSIAH, IT BEHOOVES YOU TO READ THE FOLLOWING PASSAGES OF THE BIBLE: ISAIAH 7:14, MICAH 5:2, PSALMS 72:10, JEREMIAH 31:15, HOSEA 11:1, MALACHI 3:1, ISAIAH 61:1, DEUTERONOMY 18:15, PSALMS 110:4, ISAIAH 61:1-2, PSALMS 69:7, ZACHARIAH 9:9, ISAIAH 42:1-3, PSALMS 69:9, PSALMS 78:2, ISAIAH 35:6-7, ISAIAH 8:14, PSALMS 41:9, ZECHARIAH 11:12, ZECHARIAH 13:7, PSALMS 2:1-2, ISAIAH 52:14, MICAH 5:1, ISAIAH 53:4-6, PSALMS 22:7-8, PSALMS 69:21, PSALMS 22:18, ISAIAH 53:12, PSALMS 22:1, EXODUS 12:46, ISAIAH 53:9 ZECHARIAH 12:10, PSALMS 16:10, PSALMS 68:18, PSALMS 110:1, PSALMS 45:6, PSALMS 96:1-2, 13, ISAIAH 9:6-7,

READ ALL THE ABOVE SCRIPTURES IN THE ORDER THAT THEY ARE LISTED, AND YOU WILL BE BLESSED WITH THE TRUE KNOWLEDGE THAT JESUS (YESHUA) IS **"THE MESSIAH."**

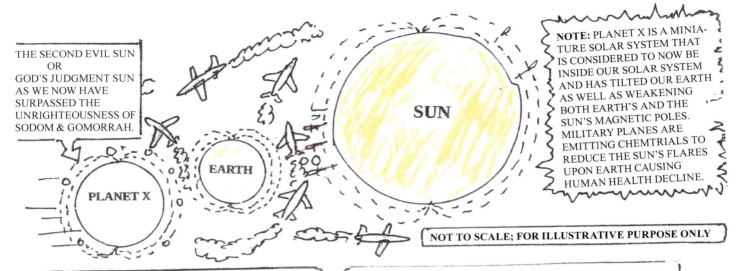

THE SECOND EVIL SUN OR GOD'S JUDGMENT SUN AS WE NOW HAVE SURPASSED THE UNRIGHTEOUSNESS OF SODOM & GOMORRAH.

NOTE: PLANET X IS A MINIATURE SOLAR SYSTEM THAT IS CONSIDERED TO NOW BE INSIDE OUR SOLAR SYSTEM AND HAS TILTED OUR EARTH AS WELL AS WEAKENING BOTH EARTH'S AND THE SUN'S MAGNETIC POLES. MILITARY PLANES ARE EMITTING CHEMTRIALS TO REDUCE THE SUN'S FLARES UPON EARTH CAUSING HUMAN HEALTH DECLINE.

NOT TO SCALE; FOR ILLUSTRATIVE PURPOSE ONLY

THE SECOND EVIL SUN HAS MANY NAMES SUCH AS PLANET X, NIBIRU, DESTROYER NEMESIS, HERCOLUBUS, RED DRAGON, MARDUK, AND IN THE BOOK OF REVELATION IT IS CALLED THE WORMWOOD.

PLANET X REALLY IS A STAR, BUT IT DOES NOT HAVE THE FUSION CAPABILITY OF OUR SUN; NEVERTHELESS, IT IS A DESTRUCTIVE STAR WITH SEVEN PLANETS ORBITING IT, AND WHEN IT DOES ORBIT OUR SUN, IT WILL CAUSE DEATH AND DESTRUCTION UPON THE EARTH.

PRESENTLY THERE ARE MILITARY MILITARY PLANES GEOENGINEERING THE SKY WITH **CHEMTRIALS** TO BLOCK THE TREMENDOUS SOLAR FLARES OF THE SUN CAUSED BY THE ENTRANCE OF PLANET X INTO OUR SOLAR SYSTEM.

PLANET X HAS CAUSED THE EARTH TO TILT MORE THAN USUAL, AND THE EARTH'S MAGNETIC FIELD IS BEGINNING TO DIMINISH. AS WELL AS THE NORTH POLE IS MOVING ABOUT 40 MILES PER YEAR TOWARD RUSSIA.

THE TREMENDOUS SOLAR FLARES EMITTING FROM THE SUN CAN CAUSE AN ELECTROMAGNETIC PULSE THAT CAN EASILY KNOCK OUT OUR GLOBAL POWER SYSTEM --- ESPECIALLY SINCE EARTH'S MAGNETIC FIELD HAS WEAKENED.

THE MAIN REASON PLANET X IS SO DESTRUCTIVE IS BECAUSE IT IS A MINIATURE SOLAR SYSTEM IN ITSELF. PLANET X HAS SEVEN PLANETS ORBITING IT AS WELL AS VARIOUS MOONS.

SURROUNDING PLANET X IS A DUST TYPE BOWL THAT MAKES IT VERY DIFFICULT TO SEE EVEN WITH AN INFRARED TELESCOPE. YET, PLANET X HAS BEEN SEEN BY THE NAKED EYE BY MANY PEOPLE ACROSS THE GLOBE WHEN SOLAR CONDITIONS ARE RIGHT.

PLANET X HAS A MAGNETIC FIELD SURROUNDING IT, WHICH MAKES IT ALL THE MORE DESTRUCTIVE TO PLANET EARTH'S MAGNETIC FIELD. RECENTLY, THE EARTH HAS LOST SOME OF ITS MAGNETIC FIELD DUE TO PLANET X ENTRANCE INTO OUR SOLAR SYSTEM.

THE SUN IS PRODUCING TREMEDOUS SOLAR FLARES AND IS THE REASON THE MILITARY PLANES ARE EMITTING CHEMTRAILS CONSISTING OF BARIUM ALUMINUM, MAGNESIUM AND OTHER CHEMICALS TO BLOCK THE SOLAR FLARE RADIATION FROM MAKING DANGEROUS CONTACT WITH THE PEOPLE ON EARTH.

RIGHT NOW ON EARTH THERE ARE ABOUT 40 TYPE VOLCANIC ERUPTIONS A DAY, ALONG WITH MANY EARTHQUAKES AROUND THE **RING OF FIRE**.

RECENT ALERTS ARE BEING MADE BY THE MANY TV STATIONS WARNING THAT THE TV MIGHT BE INTERRUPTED BY SUCH SUN SOALR FLARES.

WORTH REPEATING OVER AND OVER AGAIN IS **"DON'T BE SCARED, JUST GET PREPARED,"** JESUS (YESHUA) CONTROLS ALL THINGS AND PLACES.

YOU GET PREPARED BY (1 REPENTING (2 ACCEPTING JESUS (YESHUA) AS YOUR LORD AND SAVIOR. (3) ASKING FOR THE LORD'S HOLY SPIRIT WHO RAISED HIM FROM THE DEAD AND WILL RAPTURE YOU INTO HEAVEN ... IF AND WHEN PLANET X ORBITS OUR SUN

NOTE: Type in Planet X Physicist, Claudia Albers for confirmation about Planet X. She is harassed by NASA who falsely claims that Planet X does not exist.

Tic-Tock ... the doomsday ATOMIC CLOCK

STANDARDIZED ATOMIC CLOCK

AN ATOMIC CLOCK IS A TIME-KEEPING DEVICE WORKING VIA MOLECULAR VACILLATION, WHICH IS DIFFERENT THAN THE MECHANICAL WATCH OR CLOCK THAT HAS BALANCE WHEELS, TUNING FORKS AND PENDULUMS.

THE FIRST ATOMIC CLOCK WAS INVENTED IN 1941 USING THE VIBRATIONS OF AMMONIA MOLECULES. TODAY'S ATOMIC CLOCKS USE MORE SOPHISTICATED ATOMIC CHEMICALS FOR MORE EXACT TIME MEASUREMENTS.

ABOVE IS A **STANDARDIZED TYPE OF AN ATOMIC CLOCK**. IT ESTIMATES THAT MANKIND (ACCORDING TO ALL THE NUCLEAR BOMBS, TERRORISTS, WEATHER, AND OTHER ANOMALIES, **THE ATOMIC CLOCK SHOWS ONLY 4 MINUTES, 38 AND 6/10THS SECONDS BEFORE DOOMSDAY.** THAT IS BASED ON 24 HOURS BEING THE STANDARDIZED TIME LIMIT OF MANKIND.

PRESENTLY, A DEEP SPACE ATOMIC CLOCK IS IN PLACE AND WILL RECORD MORE EXACT TIME MEASUREMENTS. IT WAS BASED ON EINSTEIN'S THEORY THAT TIME PASSES MORE SLOWLY AT LOWER ALTITUDES. THE DEEP SPACE ATOMIC CLOCK IS 50 TIMES MORE ACCURATE FOR NOT ONLY ON EARTH, BUT, ALSO, FOR SPACE EXPLORATION.

MUCH OF TODAY'S LIFE IS BUILT AROUND THE ATOMIC CLOCK --- SUCH AS THE AUTO GPS AND SEA NAVIGATION, PRECISE CARRIER FREQUENCY FOR RADIO STATIONS, WIRELESS ALARM CLOCKS, FOR SATELLITE NAVIGATION, FOR TRACKING SPACE CRAFTS AND A MULTITUDE OF OTHER USES TECHNOLOGICALLY.

THE BOARD OF ATOMIC SCIENTISTS, BAS, DO AN ANALYSTS TEST INCLUDING ALL THE EARTHLY ABNORMAL CONDITIONS (SUCH AS NUCLEAR BOMBS, TERRORISTS, WEATHER AND OTHER SITUATION --- WHICH MIGHT VERY INCLUDE THE ADDITION OF PLANET X.

DEEP SPACE ATOMIC CLOCK

THE BOARD OF ATOMIC SCIENTISTS, BAS, ANALYZE ALL THE EARTHLY ABNORMAL CONDITIONS (SUCH AS (NUCLEAR BOMBS, TERRORISTS, WEATHER AND OTHER UNUSUAL SITUATIONS (WHICH COULD NOW VERY WELL INCLUDE PLANET X) THAT COULD PUSH THE ATOMIC CLOCK TO STRIKE THE DOOMSDAY MIDNIGHT APOCALYPSE.

THE ATOMIC CLOCK CANNOT LOSE A GAIN A SECOND IN TWENTY MILLION YEARS. SO WE HAVE PRECARIOUSLY LIVES NEARLY 98 PLUS PERCENT OF OUR EXISTENCE ON EARTH. AND PLANET X CAN END IT ALL IN A MATTER OF SECONDS ... IF AND WHEN IT DESTRUCTIVELY ORBITS OUR SUN.

HERE ARE SOME OF THE OTHER REASONS HAT THE ATOMIC CLOCK IS NEARING THE MIDNIGHT DESTRUCTION OF MANKIND.
* NUCLEAR WEAPONS.
* NORTH KOREA'S ATOMIC WEAPONS.
* NUCLEAR POWER PLANTS
* DIRTY NANOTECHNOLOGY BOMBS.
* GLOBAL WARS GEARING UP.
* SEVERE VOLCANOES, EARTHQUAKES.
* OVER GROWTH OF POPULATION.
* INADEQUATE ENERGY RESOURCES.
* LACK OF DRINKING WATER.
* PLANET X DESTROYS PLANET EARTH.

THE ABOVE LISTED CONDITIONS CAN END MANKIND'S EXISTENCE ON EARTH.

PLEASE NOTE THAT THE ATOMIC CLOCK DOES NOT INCLUDE SPIRITUAL AND OR THEOLOGICAL ASPECTS OF STRIKING "MIDNIGHT."

The Judgment Seat Atomic Clock

PEOPLE SHOULD KEEP THEIR EYE ON THE FOUR MINUTES AND SOME SECONDS LEFT ON THE "MANKIND'S ATOMIC CLOCK" THAT SIGNALS THE POTENTIAL ANNIHILATION OF HUMAN LIFE.

BUT EVEN MORE IMPORTANT IS BEING ACUTELY AWARE OF ALMIGHTY GOD'S "JUDGMENT ATOMIC CLOCK" THAT WILL DETERMINE WHO OBTAINS ETERNAL LIFE.

OTHER PREVIOUS CIVILIZATIONS DID NOT BELIEVE IN THE LORD GOD, AND THEY LED A LIFE OF UNRIGHTEOUSNESS. THEIR OBSESSION WITH SIN AND EVIL SET THE STAGE FOR THEIR ABRUPT ENDING OF LIFE HERE ON EARTH.

TODAY, THE WORLD IS ALSO OBSESSED WITH EVIL IN THE FORMS OF --- ABORTION (IMMOLATION), LAWLESSNESS, ADULTERY, FORNICATION, WICKED GOSSIP, SLOTH, DRUG INFESTATION, EMBEZZLEMENTS, IDOLATRY, STEALING, BRIBES, MURDER, IMMORAL SEX, CHEATING, LYING, GREED, DEMONIC POSSESSION, FOUL LANGUAGE, ALONG WITH A HOST OF OTHER WAYS OF THINKING, SPEAKING AND LIVING.

FATHER GOD HAS GIVEN US HIS ONLY BEGOTTEN SON, JESUS CHRIST (YESHUA) AS THE LORD AND SAVIOR WHO OFFERS A SINNER **GRACE** (UNMERITED FAVOR) AND MERCY (UNDESERVED FORGIVENESS) OF OUR SINS. ALL WE HAVE TO DO IS (1) REPENT OF OUR SINS, (2) ACCEPT JESUS AS OUR LORD AND SAVIOR AND (3) ASK FOR HIS HOLY SPIRIT TO ENTER INTO YOUR HEART, MIND, SOUL AND SPIRIT..

PLEASE REMEMBER, HOWEVER, THAT REPENTING DOES NOT JUST MEAN YOU ARE SORRY FOR YOUR SINS, IT MEANS YOU ARE MAKING A SPIRITUAL DECISION **TO CHANGE** YOUR WAY OR LIVING.

"MOST OF THE PROBLEMS IN THIS WORLD ARE CAUSED BY THOSE FALLEN ANGELS CALLED DEMONS."

"WOE"

"WE ARE FINISHED PRETTY MUCH WITH THE BROWN DWARF STAR AND ITS SEVEN ORBITING PLANETS. JUDEO/CHRISTIAN BELIEVERS KNOW FROM THE BOOK OF REVELATION CHAPTERS 5 THROUGH 22, THAT THE EVIL ONES ON EARTH WILL BE JUDGED BY AN APOCALYPTIC FALLING OF STARS METEORITES, COMETS, EARTHQUAKES, AND VIOLENT WIND AND STORMS."

"IT MAY NOT BE PLANET X ... BUT YOU CAN BE SURE IT WILL BE SOME KIND OF PLANET OR STAR THAT PLUMMETS EARTH"

"BUT, AS THE LORD, JESUS CHRIST, SAID, "ONLY FATHER GOD KNOWS THE HOUR AND DAY OF THE END-TIME APOCALYPSE. SHOWN BELOW ARE THE SEVEN SEALS, THE SEVEN TRUMPETS, AND THE SEVEN BOWLS OF WRATH AT THE END TIMES."

"THIS IS REALLY SCARY, ROSCOE, BUT RIGHTEOUSLY JUSTIFIED."

THE SEVEN SEALS ... AND THEIR MEANING.

WHITE HORSE (CONQUER) — THE SACRIFICIAL LAMB, CHRIST JESUS, BREAKS OPEN THE SEAL AND A RIDER ON A WHITE HORSE GOES OUT TO CONQUER ALL.

RED HORSE (WAR) — THE SECOND SEAL BRINGS A RIDER ON A RED HORSE WHO CAUSES MEN TO KILL EACH OTHER IN WAR.

BLACK HORSE FAMINE — THE THIRD SEAL HAS A RIDER ON A BLACK HORSE WHO BRINGS FAMINE AND DEATH.

PALE HORSE (DEATH) — THE FOURTH SEAL HAS A RIDER ON A PALE HORSE WHO IS CALLED "DEATH AND HADES."

THE MARTYRS (REVENGE) — THE FIFTH SEAL UNCOVERS THE MANY MARTYRS WHO ARE TOLD TO REST A WHILE LONGER BEFORE JUDGMENT.

EARTHQUAKE THE SUN, STARS MOON FALL. — THE SIXTH SEAL BRINGS EARTH-QUAKES AND AND THE SUN BECOMES BLACK AND THE STARS FALL FROM THE SKY.

SEVEN TRUMPETS GIVEN TO ANGELS — THE SEVENTH SEAL HAS FIRE, HAIL AND BLOOD. GOD'S REVENGE IS JUST AS HE JUDGES THOSE WHO KILLED HIS PEOPLE.

THE SEVEN RUMPETS ... AND THEIR MEANING.

HAIL, FIRE, AND BLOOD DESTROY THE EARTH.

A MOUNTAIN OF FIRE IS TOSSED INTO THE SEA DESTROYING SHIPS ANDS LIFE.

THE WORMWOOD STAR FALLS FROM THE SKY THAT DESTROYS THE DRINKING WATER AND MUCH LIFE.

ONE THIRD OF THE SUN, MOON AND STARS BECOME BLACK AND UNSTEADY.

AN ANGEL OPENS THE BOTTOMLESS PIT RELEASING THE SCORPION LIKE LOCUSTS THAT ENDLESSLY STING MANKIND.

FOUR BAD ANGELS RELEASED FROM THE EUPHRATES RIVER AND KILL ONE THIRD OF MANKIND.

THE KINGDOM OF THE WORLD IS NOW AND FOREVER THE KINGDOM OF ALMIGHTY GOD.

THE SEVEN BOWLS OF WRATH ... AND THEIR MEANINGG.

THE SCORCHING SUN RAISES EVIL SORES ON ... ALL WHO HAVE THE 666 MARK OF THE BEAST ON THEM.

THE BLOOD OF THE DEAD IS POURED INTO THE SEA AND MANY DIE FROM THE LACK OF WATER.

THE EVIL ONES ARE MADE TO DRINK OF THE BLOOD OF THE DEAD WHICH IS BITTER AND ODIOUS.

AGAIN THE RELENTLESS SUN SCORCHES THE EVIL ONES LEFT ON THE EARTH.

THEN THE BOWL OF WRATH IS POURED ON SATAN'S THRONE SIGNIFYING HIS END ON EARTH.

THE BOWL OF WRATH IS POURED INTO THE EUPHRATES RIVER AND SATAN, THE BEAST AND ANTICHRIST ARE TOSSED INTO THE PIT OF FIRE AND SULFUR.

THEN THE ANGELS SING IN GLORY, "IT IS DONE!" AND A NEW HEAVEN AND A NEW EARTH IS ESTABLISHED FOR GOD'S PEOPLE.

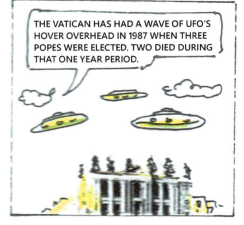

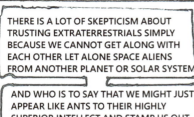

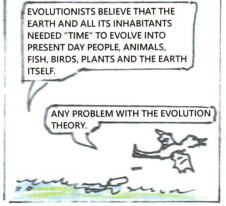
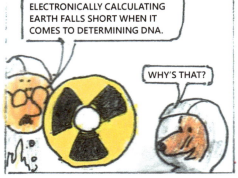

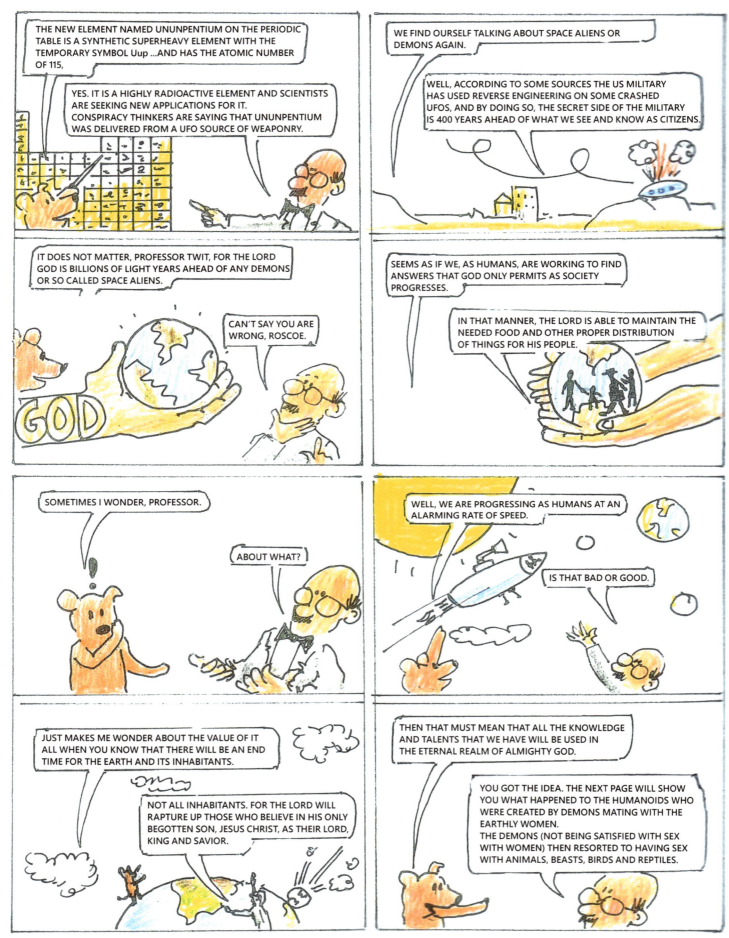

The Book of Enoch was found written in the "Dead Sea Scrolls."

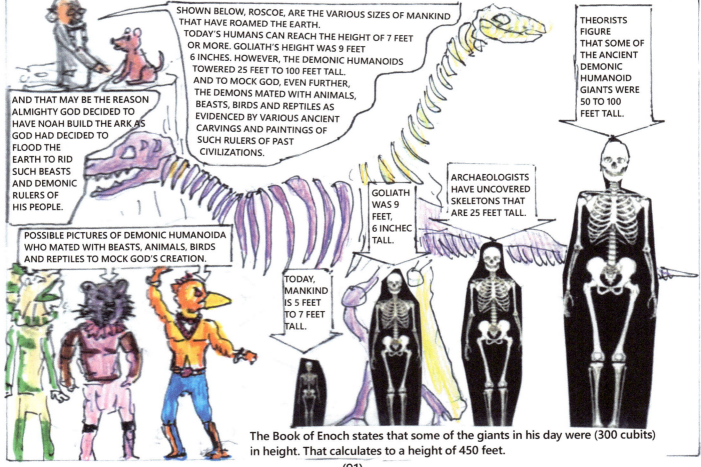

The Book of Enoch states that some of the giants in his day were (300 cubits) in height. That calculates to a height of 450 feet.

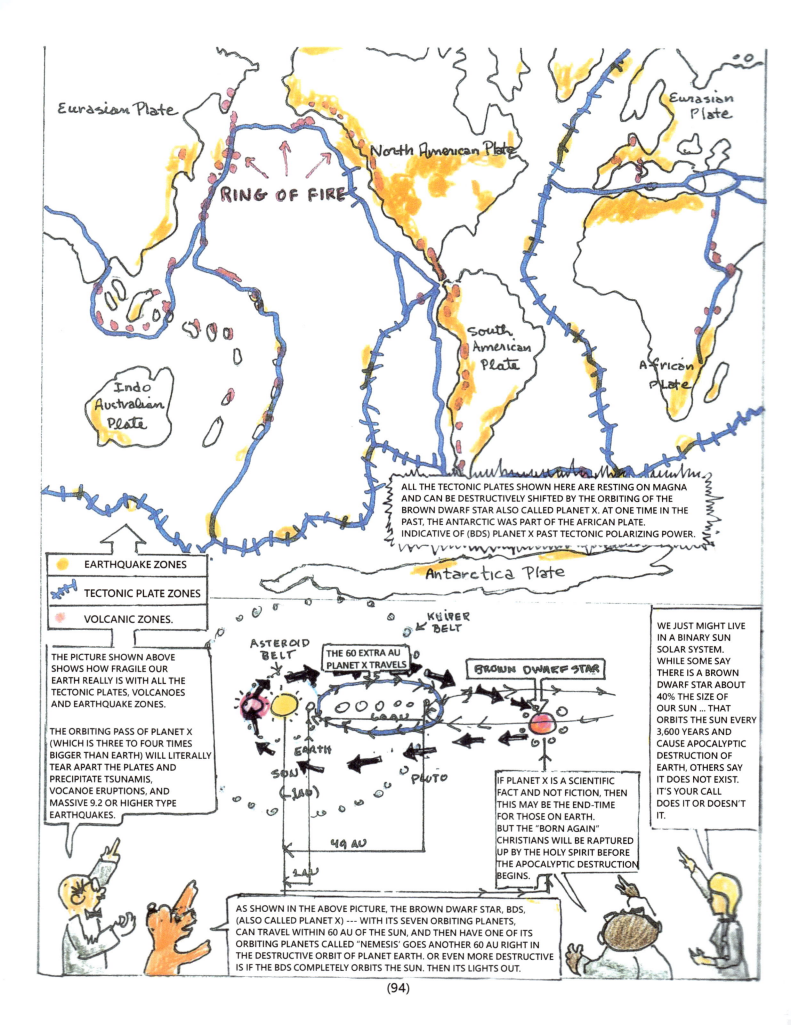

TECTONIC PLATE

JON ANDERSON, FORMERLY OF NASA SAYS THE PLANET X (NIBIRU) HAS A MASS ABOUT 5 TIMES THE SIZE OF EARTH.
THE AUSTRALIAN AUTHOR, STEPHANIE RELFE IS CONVINCED THAT THERE IS A CONSPIRACY SURROUNDING PLANE X IN ALL GOVERNMENTS.
PLANET EARTH, IN 1990, HAS ALREADY EXPERIENCED TECTONIC PLATE MOVEMENTS EVIDENCED BY THE INDONESIAN EARTHQUAKE TSUNAMI AND JAPAN HAS ALSO EXPERIENCED THE RECENT TSUNAMI.
IF THERE IS A PLANET X (NIBIRU) ORBIT CLOSE TO EARTH, IT WILL DISRUPT EARTH'S TECTONIC PLATES CAUSING, VOCANIC ERUPTIONS, EARTHQUAKES TORNADOES, HIGH VELOCITY WINDS, GAS PIPE LINE BREAKAGE, NUCLEAR EXPLOSIONS SOLAR EQUIPMENT BREAKDOWN, SATELLITES OUT OF ORDER, POWER BLACK OUTS. NO HEAT OR AIR CONDITIONING, THE EARTH WILL WOBBLE AND MANY WILL DIE FROM THE SOLAR FLARES AND EXHAUSTING HEAT. AND THE MOON, SUN AND STARS WILL TURN BLACK AND PLANETS, ASTEROIDS, COMETS WILL FLY UNCONTROLLABLY IN THE SKY.

VOLCANO

THERE ARE ABOUT 1,500 KINDS OF ACTIVE VOLCANOES IN THE WORLD.
MOST OF THE VOLCANOES ARE AROUND THE RING OF FIRE, LOCATED ALONG THE PACIFIC RIM.
YOUNG SEA FLOOR VOLCANOES ARE IN THE MILLIONS.
VOLCANOES HELP KEEP THE EARTH COOL, BUILDING MATERIALS, ROADS NUCLEAR AND MORE

EARTHQUAKE

THERE ARE AROUND 14,000 EARTHQUAKES A YEAR WORLD WIDE.
THAT'S ABOUT 40 EARTHQUAKES A DAY.
THE SHIFT IN TECTONIC PLATES CAUSE EARTHQUAKES, ALONG WITH VOLCANOES AND TSUNAMI IF PLANET X ORBITS NEAR PLANET EARTH THERE WILL BE MASSIVE TECTONIC PLATE SHIFTS.

TSUNAMI

THE WORLD'S TALLEST TSUNAMI 1,720 FEET HIGH WAS RECORDED IN LITUYA BAY, ALASKA.
MANY THOUSANDS OF PLACES HAVE BEEN DESTROYED BY TSUNAMI. (TO NAME FEW) SUCH AS 373 HELIKE, GREECE. 79 AD GULF OF NAPLES, ITALY, 1303 CRETE, 1868 HAWAIIAN ISLANDS, 1929 NEW FOUNDLAND, 1958 ALASKA, USA, 2004 INDIAN OCEAN, 2007 JAPAN.
IF PLANET X (NIBIRU) ORBITS CLOSE TO EARTH, IT WILL CAUSE TREMENDOUSLY HUGE TSUNAMI. WHICH WILL COMPLETELY INUNDATE ALL THE UNDERGROUND BUNKERS BUILT AROUND THE WORLD ALONG WITH THE HIGH TSUNAMI WILL BE DESTRUCTIVE TORNADOES HIGH VIOLENT WINDS WITH ERUPTIONS OF ALL INFRASTRUCTURES. LIFE AS WE KNOW IT WILL NOT EXIST.

FATHER GOD YAHWEH, I DO NOT KNOW WHAT LIES AHEAD TOMORROW TO MYSELF OR THE GROUND UPON WHICH I WALK, BUT I AM SURE THAT I NEED YOUR FORGIVENESS THROUGH YOUR ONLY BEGOTTEN SON, JESUS CHRIST. SO I ASK YOU, JESUS, TO FORGIVE ME OF MY SINS IN MY UNRIGHTEOUS THOUGHTS, WORDS AND DEEDS. YOU ARE MY LORD, KING, SAVIOR, BROTHER, DIVINE PHYSICIAN, HIGH PRIEST, COUNSELOR, AND PROTECTOR. THE SACRIFICIAL LAMB FOR THE FORGIVENESS OF ALL SINS FOR ALL ETERNITY. AND I ASK FOR YOUR HOLY SPIRIT TO BE SPIRITUALLY "BORN AGAIN;" FOR YOUR SPIRIT OF WISDOM TO JUDGE CORRECTLY AND FOR THE PROTECTION OF YOUR ANGELS AND ARCHANGELS. AND I THANK YOU FOR GOING UNTO FATHER GOD YAHWEH TO INTERCEDE FOR ME, FOR YOU ARE ONE IN BEING WITH HIM. THANK YOU, JESUS FOR SAVING ME, MY FAMILY, FRIENDS, RELATIVES, AND THE PEOPLE OF THE WORLD BOTH PAST AND PRESENT. AND LORD MY PRAYERS ARE ALSO FOR THE LOST WHO NEVER HAD THE OPPORTUNITY TO KNOW OF YOUR SAVING MERCY AND GRACE.

SATAN ALREADY KNOWS WHAT IS ABOUT TO HAPPEN. AND HE IS PARANOID ABOUT BEING BETRAYED.
FOR THE DEVIL KNOWS ALL THE APOSTLES WERE BETRAYED AND EVEN JESUS WAS BETRAYED
SO SATAN WILL MAKE SURE ALL THE PEOPLE LEFT ON THE EARTH HAVE THE INFAMOUS 666 PUT ON THEIR FOREHEAD R HAND. FOR HE KNOWS THAT ALL WHO RECEIVE HIS 666 MARK CANNOT EVER GET INTO HEAVEN, AND WILL THEREBY SERVE HIM IN TOTAL FEAR AND SUBSERVANCY.

WOE, WOE UNTO YOU, YOU DEMONS WHO KNOW OF GOD YET MOCK HIM WITH YOUR DEMONIC DEEDS UPON THE EARTH, FOR THE LORD JESUS CHRIST COMES WITH HIS ANGELS FILLED WITH WRATH AND INDIGNATION AND WILL CAST ALL OF YOU INTO THE PIT OF FIRE AND SULFUR ... FOREVER AND EVER WORLD WITHOUT END.

WOE, WOE UNTO YOU INHABITANTS OF THE EARTH WHO FOLLOW THE WAY OF THE EVIL ONE, FOR YOU WILL BE CAST OUTSIDE THE GATES OF HEAVEN WHERE YOU WILL WAIL AND GNASH YOUR TEETH AN GREAT ANGUISH AND DISPAIR. FOREVER DEPARTED FROM FATHER GOD.

AND WOE, WOE UNTO YOU, SATAN, THE BEAST AND ANTICHRIST, FOR THE RIGHT HAND OF GOD COMES WITH FIRE AND BRIMSTONE AND YOU WILL BE CAST INTO THE LAKE OF FIRE AND SULFUR WHERE YOU WILL BE IN TORTURE, AS YOU TORTURED THE LORD'S PEOPLE, FOREVER AND EVER WORLD WITHOUT END.

AND ABANDON ALL HOPE YE WHO ENTRANCE INTO THE PIT OF HELL.

HERE IS AN OUTLINE OF WHAT YOU READ SO FAR.

TOPIC	EXPLANATION	PAGE

(1) ANCIENT HISTORY OF PLANET X:
The Sumerians (now called Iraq) including Babylon and Mesopotamia were the first civilization to invent writing math, science, medicine, astronomy, and other fields of earning. The Russian scientist, Zechariah Sitchin, wrote about alleged aliens (or demons) whom he called tAnunnaki." He sold 20 million copies of his book titled "The 12th Planet,' but scientists judged the book to b fraudulent." Nevertheless Sitchin stated that the 12th Planet would return every 3,600 years. A date and time that humankind falls below the unrighteousness of Sodom and Gomorrah. Other scientists do say, "Planet X is overdue and males its entry int our Solar System every 2, 300 to 3,000 years. If Planet X orbits our Sun, then its "Lights Out" for Planet Earth as it will set off the thousands of volcanoes and the apocalypse occurs. Don't be scared. Just get prepared, Accept Jesus as your Savior and you will be saved and taken into Heaven...76

(2) THE SUMERIAN STONE TABLET FEATURES THE 12 PLANETS AND DATA ABOUT THE ANUNNAKI:
The number 12 has other Sumerian implications such as there 12 inches n a foot, 12 eggs in a dozen, 12 hours of daylight and 12 hours of night, 12 tribes if Israel. 12 Disciples, 12 signs of the Zodiac, 12 Greek Olympians, Planet z is supposedly 20% the size of or sun, and is located just outside our Sun, and was recorded on the Sumerian Stone Tablet 6,000 years ago. Planet X is still within the gravitational pull of our Sun 77

(3) WORLD WIDE RETURN OF THE JEWS TO ISRAEL:
In Isaiah 43:5-6, The Prophet Isaiah said from the East the Jews will return to Israel from the Arab countries. From the West the Jews will return to Israel from Germany. From the North, the Jews will return to Israel from Russia. From the South, the Jews will return to Israel from Ethiopia but a ransom is paid to release them.
NOTE: Under the Old Testament, the Israelites lived under LAW. But under the New Testament, the Israelites live under Jesus' MERCY (undeserved forgiveness) and Jesus' GRACE (unmerited Favor). The law allowed Satan to incarcerate the Jews, bu9t Jesus Mercy and Grace provides the forgiveness the Israelites now enjoy and are not tricked into damnation by the devil..................78

(99)

(4) CHEMTRAIL PLANES ARE CIRCULATING THE EARTH:
Planet X is a miniature Solar system with a few planets and moons orbiting it. Allegedly The United Nations has awarded $50 Billion to fly Chemtrail Planes around the Earth to stop the Sun's Solar Flares from hitting Earth causing damage to airports and other important facilities Planet x is also causing Earthquakes, floods, and could knock out the our Global Power System.
NOTE: The chemicals in the Chemtrail Planes are Aluminum, Barium, Magnesium and other deadly chemicals that are causing cancer, Alzheimer and other death type diseases to humankind

as well as to animals, birds, etc. Don't be scared Just get prepared. Ask Jesus to save you 79

(5) TIC-TOCK ... THE DOOMSDAY ATOMIC CLOCK.
The Atomic Clock works by molecular vacillation which is different then the mechanical clock that has balance wheel, tuning forks and a pendulums. The first Atomic Clock was invented in 1941, and today's Atomic Clock is more sophisticated and has perfect timing. The Deep Space Atomic Clock is even more accurate. Today's Atomic Clock cannot lose or gain a second in twenty million years. Right now, the Atomic Clock shows that only 4 minutes. 38 and 6/10th seconds before DOOMSDAY. This Doomsday figure is based on the following things potentially happening: Planet X orbits our Sun, proliferation of Nuclear Weapons, Nuclear Power Plants, Dirty Nanotechnology Bombs, Severe Volcano Ruptures, Lack of Food and Drinking Water, and

other global mishaps 80

(6) GOD'S JUDGMENT SEAT ATOMIC CLOCK:
Either the Global Community REPENTS of Abortion, Immolation, Adultery, Lawlessness, Fornication, Embezzlement, Drugs, Sloth, Murder, Lying, Bribes, Demonic Possession, Foul Language, Idolatry, Greed and other forms of evilness, or Almighty God will destroy tod ay;s

civilization as he did with past immoral and ungodly civilizations 81

(7) QUESTION; IS ALL THAT YOU HAVE READ SO FAR FACT, FICTION, RELIGION OR SCIENCE? YOU DECIDE.

                FACT   RELIGION

                SCIENCE   FICTION

Careful now. You are the Judge which takes Honorable Discernment 82

(100)

(8) **THIS PAGE IS A SYNOPSIS OF THE BOOK OF REVELATION AND IS A GOOD TOOL TO USE WHEN READING ABOUT THE 7 SEALS, THE 7 TRUMPETS, AND THE 7 BOWLS OF WRATH.**
Do read the Book of Revelation and refer to the chart 83

(9) **SPACE ALIENS (WHO ARE REALLY DEMONIC ENTITIES) ARE IN CONTACT WITH POLITICIANS AND RELIGIOUS LEADERS TO SET UP THE ONE WORLD ORDER:**
The Satanic Entities are intelligent enough to place a Hologram across the sky to fool the global community that it is Christ's return. Only the very Elect of the Lord God's people will know it is a fake, as Satan comes first to fool the people into worshiping him. Be aware that Satan precedes Jesus' Return. Father God allows this as He has forewarned His Elect of this Global Satanic Charade.

(10) **SATANIC FORCES WILL PLACE A HOLOGRAM IN THE SKY (LOOKING LIKE CHRIST) IN EACH COUNTRY TO SET THE STAGE TO FOOL THE GLOBAL COMMUNITY INTO WORSHIPING HIM:**
The intellect of the Satanic Forces is sufficient to fool a multitude of the billions of people 84

(11) **GOD'S SPIRITUAL FINGERPRINTS ARE ON EVERYONE'S DNA, PURPOSE IN LIFE, PROTECTION, AND THEIR LIFESPAN:**
God even protects Earth from asteroids, but will allow and asteroid to hit Earth if the global Community falls below the unrighteous of Sodom & Gomorrah 85

(12) **SCRIPTURES THAT CONFIRM THAT JESUS CHRIST IS THE ONLY BEGOTTEN SON OF FATHER GOD AND IS THE ONLY TRUE MESSIAH AND SAVIOR OF THE PEOPLE ON EARTH:**
The Biblical Scriptures on this page feature the Old Testament Prophets and how Jesus Christ fulfilled each one in its exact order in time and sequence, ... 86

(13) EVEN THE HOPI INDIANS HAVE THEIR "SIGNS" OF A GREAT HAPPENING WILL MAKE THE EARTH ROCK BACK AND FORTH AND STRANGE BEASTS WILL WALK ON THE EARTH AND VIOLENT WINDS AND VOLCANOES AND EARTHQUAKES WILL DEVASTATE THE EARTH.
This pages is not something to make the Elect of God to fear, as they will be taken up beforehand. It does however, show where different nationalities and different Ethnic Groups also have their signs of the End Time 87

(14) IS THE EARTH AND UNIVERSE DUE TO EVOLUTION OR CREATION ... OR A BIT OF BOTH IN THAT EARTH IS 6,000 YEARS, BUT GOD IS EON (UNFATHOMABLE) IN TIME.
Many scientists believe that humankind did not evolve from monkeys or apes or any other microorganism. On the other hand, there are scientists that do believe Humankind stems from other animal like creatures and microorganisms. It's your call Read and see what you come up with 88

(15) THE MILITARY LOCATED AT AREA 51 (NEVADA) ARE SUPPOSEDLY 400 YEARS AHEAD OF THE OTHER SCIENTISTS ON EARTH,
This page shows how reverse engineering of crashed Alien-Like Crafts (or Satanic type UFO's) have greatly enhanced the technological ability of the secret Area 51 Scientists inH Nevada. Word has it that they even had a live member 89

(16) WHEN THE FALLEN ANGELS WERE TOSSED OUT OF HEAVEN AND ONTO EARTH, THEY ALLEGEDLY OR POSITIVELY COHABITED WITH THE WOMEN ON EARTH AS WELL AS WITH ANIMALS, BIRDS ETC.
According to Enoch (of the Old Testament) the Human Cohabitants were 50 feet tall and even higher. God destroyed the co called "Nihilism" Giants and the Animal/Bird, and Serpent Giant-Like Creatures via Noah's Flood. This is a rather difficult part of the Bible to believe, so they did not put Enoch's Story in the Bible ... but it does not make it untrue. The Devil tries to imitate everything God creates 90

(17) THIS PAGE SHOWS THE HORROR OF HELL:
Jesus and His Angels toss the Demons and Demonic Entities into the lake of Fire & Su9lfur....... 91

(18) A COLORFUL (CARICATURE) PICTURE OF THE MILKY WAY GALAXY:
This features Professor Twit, Roscoe, Dr. Newt, and Dr. Tamar viewing the Milky Way Galaxy 92

(19) THE RING OF FIRE VOLCANOES ARE ALWAYS A THREAT TO THE PEOPLE ON PLANET EARTH. ESPECIALLY IF "PLANET X" ORBITS OUR SUN
If the Global Community does not repent of its unrighteous ways, the Lord God will have "Planet X" orbit our Sun and the Sun will turn black, the moon will lose its light, and the asteroids (between Mars and Jupiter) will devastatingly plummet the Earth..93

(20) THE WAYS (VOLCANOES, EARTHQUAKES, TSUNAMI, AND THE SHIFTING TECTONIC PLATES CAN APOCALYPTIC DESTROY EARTH.
If the thousands of volcanoes explode then the Tectonic Plates will shift thousands of mile apart, and Planet Earth will become desolate 94

(21) THE 15th CENTURY CARDINAL BISHOP OF TUSCULUM ESTIMATED THAT 1/3rd OF THE FALLEN ANGELS FROM HEAVEN REPRESENTED ABOUT 133,306,668 OF THEM:
God also chained many of the fallen angels iunder the Earth 95

(22) PRESIDENT TRUMAN DEVELOPED THE "MAJESTIC 12" TO UNCOVER WHAT IS OCCURRING ONE EARTH DUE TO FALLEN ANGELS OR OTHER STRANGE ENTITIES;
One of the Majestic 12, named James Forrestal, leaked something of the Majestic 12 information and was placed into a mental Institution where he died expectantly 96

(23) SATAN KIDNAPS HUMANS AND PUTS THEM UNDER OBSERVATION AND SURGERY TO FIND OUT HOW THEY THINK IN RELATION TO GOD.
It has been told that former President Eisenhower traded humans to (in return) for technological data 97

FROM ADAM TO THE NOAH'S FLOOD

The time span from Adam to Noah's Flood was 1,656 years which included ten generations. The population during Noah's time was around 170 million people.

Now some statisticians (who add on the exponentiation factor) think that the global population during Noah's Flood was around 4 billion people.

Let's see, you had Adam, then Seth, Enos, Cainan, Mahalaleel, Jared, Enoch, Methuselah, Lamech, and Noah to populate the globe to either 179 million or 4 billion people.

What bothers and makes theological statisticians concerned is the time period between Noah and Jesus which is 4,000 years.

If you add on today's date of 2024, you come up with the time period from Noah to Jesus today being 6,024 years. That has theologians very concerned about the END TIME.

Not only did God rid the world of sinful people during Noah's time, He also had fire and brimstone fall upon Sodom &, Gomorrah, God also had the Earth swallow up Dathan, Abraim, and Korah's families for not obeying Moses orders.

IN 1776 THE AMERICAN THE 13 COLONIES OF AMERICA SEVERED THEIR POLITICAL TIES WITH GREAT BRITAIN.

Just think of the bravado of the bravado of the men like George Washington, Alexander Hamilton, Thomas Jefferson to name a few who only had 13 colonies with a population of only around 3 million going to war with Great Britain who had an 8 million population and an army the very size of all of the 13 colonies.

God must have had a hand in the establishment of America.

Today America is divided into the Red States and the Blue States. Not everyone in the Blue States is evil, and not everyone in the Red States are good.

I do wonder, however, if the people of the United States of America want to keep sovereign from the Satanic One World Order.

We have to pattern our courage like our historic forefathers if we intend to live free and independent from the captivity of a very restrictive world-wide government that can limit our freedom hundreds of times more than Great Britain placed upon our forefathers.

How do you do this. Jesus vote for the leader who offers you the best freedom from Satanic forces.

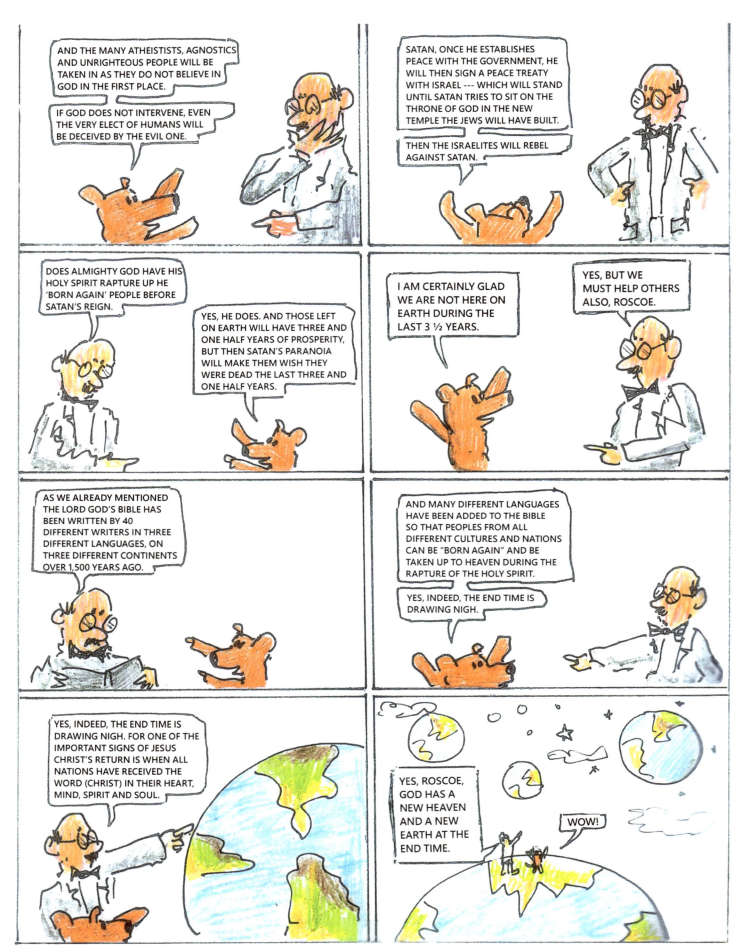

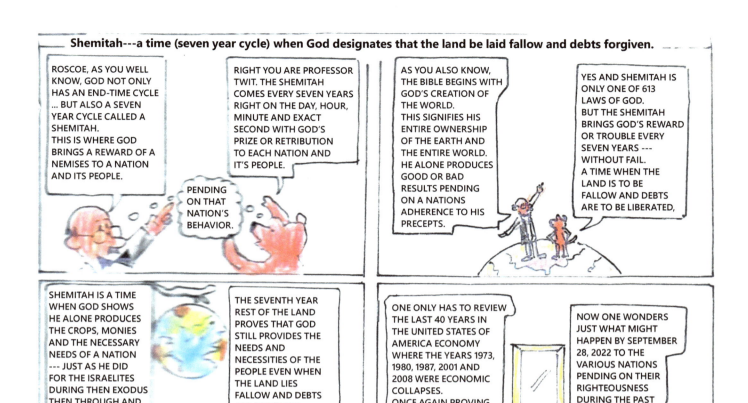

The Four Jewish Holy Day Blood Moon and Two Solar Eclipses in 2014 & 2015

SHOWN HERE, ROSCOE, ARE TWO SOLAR AND FOUR LUNAR ECLIPSES WHICH HAVE OCCURRED ON JEWISH HOLY DAYS. AND NO OTHER SOLAR OR LUNAR ECLIPSES HAVE OCCURRED DURING THIS TIME PERIOD. SOMETHING BIG IS GOING TO HAPPEN IN SEPTEMBER 2022

| 15 April 2024 Jewish Passover Eclipse | 8 Oct 2014 Feast of Tabernacle Eclipse | 20 March 2015 Jewish New Years for Kings Eclipse | 4 April 2015 Jewish Passover Eclipse | 13 Sept 2015 Feast of Trumpets Eclipse | 28 Sept 2015 Feast of Tabernacle Eclipse |

THE SEVEN JEWISH HOLY DAYS ARE:

1. PASSOVER
2. UNLEAVENED BREAD
3. FIRST FRUITS
4. PENECOST
5. TRUMPETS (ROSH HASHANAH)
6. ATONEMENT (YOM KIPPUR)
7. TABERNACLES

AND HANUKKAH IS ALSO CELEBRATED

HOW JEWISH AND CHRISTIAN HOLY DAYS COINCIDE IN 2015

JEWISH HOLY DAY	DATE	CELEBRATION	CHRISTIAN HOLY DAY	CELEBRATION
PASSOVER	4-3-15	Lamb's blood set them free	JESUS ON THE CROSS	Jesus' shed blood salvation.
UNLEAVENED BREAD	4-4-15	No leaven (sin) in eaten bread	JESUS DIED WITHOUT SIN	Jesus is the epitome of no sin.
FIRST FRUITS	4-5-15	First crops offered to God	JESUS IS THE FIRST FRUIT	Jesus is the First Fruit from dead.
PENTECOST	7-31-15	The Law Fifty days after Passover	JESUS OVERCOMES THE LAW	Apostles meet 50 days after Passover
ROSH HASHANAH	9-16-15	Jews celebrate New Year	JESUS BEGINS HIS REIGN	Jesus amidst trumpets appears.
YOM KIPPUR	9-23-15	Atonement for past sins	JESUS' ATONES FOR ALL SIN	Jesus mercy & grace atones all sin.
TABERNACLES	12-7-15	Jews build small tabernacles	JESUS IS THE ETERNAL ARK	Jesus is the eternal Tabernacle/

ANOTHER JEWISH HOLIDAY IS HANUKKAH: (December 7, 2015) in which the candle flame (light) kept burning. The Christians celebrate Christmas (December 25, 2015) as Jesus is the "Eternal Light." **The book life and death will be read someday between Rosh Hashanah and Yom kippur.**

Scientists, theologians, astronomers, thought leaders and others say, "The End Time is not a matter of 'if' But 'when.'" And every seven years the Lord God emits the "Shemitah" rewarding or punishing nations.

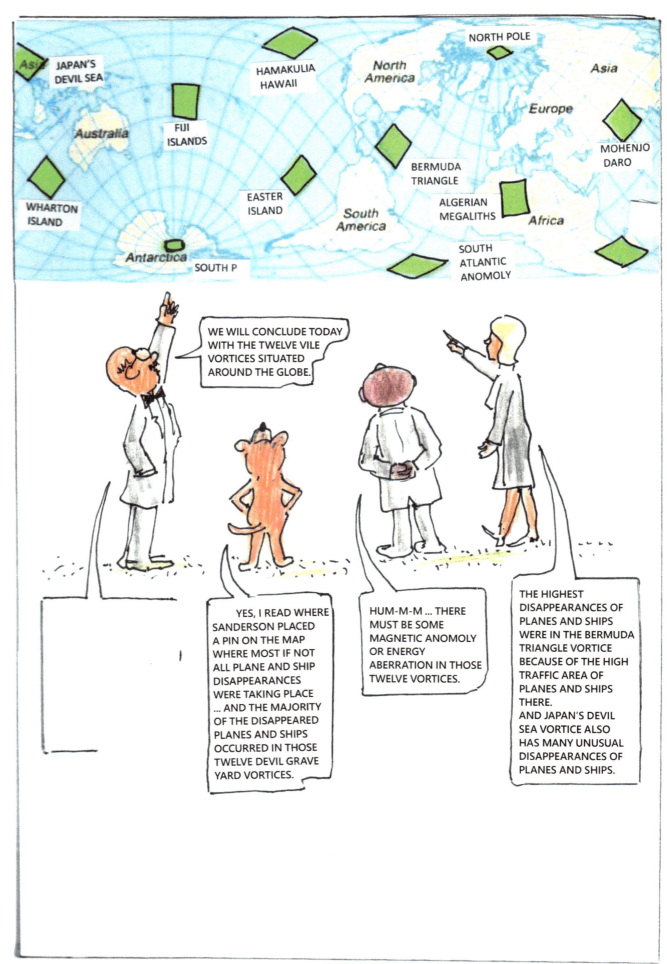
(108)

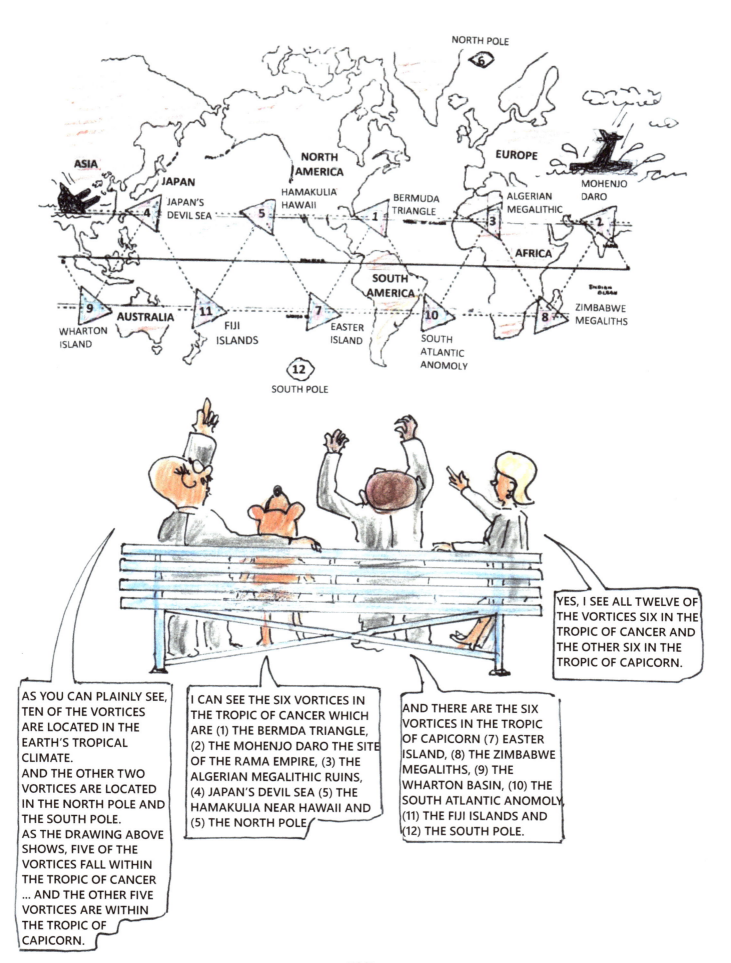

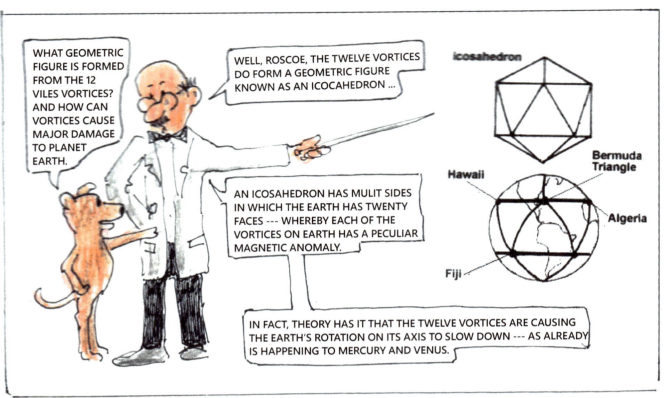

Admiral Byrd's South Pole Vortices' Expedition

IN 1947 PRESIDENT HARRY TRUMAN ASSEMBLED A PANEL OF 12 MEN TO EXAMINE UFO'S AND OTHER PHENOMINA OCCURING AROUND THE WORLD. THE 12 MEN PANEL WAS CALLED THE "MAJESTIC TWELVE."

THROUGH TRUMAN'S COMMAND, JAMES FORRESTAL, THEN SECRETARY OF DEFENSE, COMMISSIONED ADMIRAL BYRD (WITH A FLOTILLA OF 40 SHIPS AND 1,400 SAILORS) TO EXAMINE THE SOUTH POLE VORTICE --- UNDER THE GUISE OF DISCOVERING NEW MATERIALS AND OTHER MADE-UP EXCUSES.

THE REAL REASON FOR ADMIRAL BYRD'S EXPEDITION WAS TO SEE IF POST-WAR NAZI WAR STATIONS WERE SET UP IN THE SOUTH POLE VORTICE.

UPON ENTERING THE SOUTH POLE VORTICE, ADMIRAL BYRD WAS UNDER ATTACK FROM UFO'S AND OTHER OUT-OF-THIS--WORLD WAR ARMAMENT. IN CONCERN HE MIGHT LOSE HIS ENTIRE FLEET, ADMIRAL BYRD RETREATED BACK TO AMERICA WHERE HE REPORTED THE MIGHTY ALIEN-LIKE ATTACK ... BUT HIS REPORT WAS BLACKBALLED AND STUFFED AWAY.

LATER BOTH JAMES FORRESTAL AND ADMIRAL BYRD WANTED TO EXPLAIN TO THE PUBLIC OF THE STRANGE AND POWERFUL FORCE, BUT BOTH DIED. SOME SAY BOTH OF THEM WERE EVENTUALLY MURDERED TO KEEP THEIR REPORTS CONFIDENTIAL.

JAPAN'S DEVIL'S SEA VORTICE (DRAGON'S TRIANGLE)

THE JAPAN DEVIL'S SEA (ALSO CALLED THE DRAGON'S TRIANGLE) IS OF GRAVE CONCERN TO THE JAPAN GOVERNMENT.
BETWEEN THE YEARS 1952 TO 1954, FIVE JAPANESE MILITARY VESSELS WERE LOST IN THE TRIANGLE WITH 700 PERSONNEL ABOARD.
THEN THE JAPAN GOVERNMENT FUNDED A TEAM OF 100 SCIENTISTS ABOARD THE EXPEDITION OF THE VESSEL KAIYO MARU WHICH ALSO DISAPPEARED.
NOW ONE WONDERS IF THE MALAYSIAN FLIGHT MH370 ALSO MET WITH A SIMILAR DISASTER. DID AMELIA EARHART ALSO DISAPPEAR THERE IN 1937?

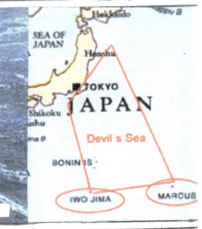

Tectonic plate shifts can also sink ships by causing a tsunamis or a rogue wave.

THE BERMUDA TRIANGLE VORTICE

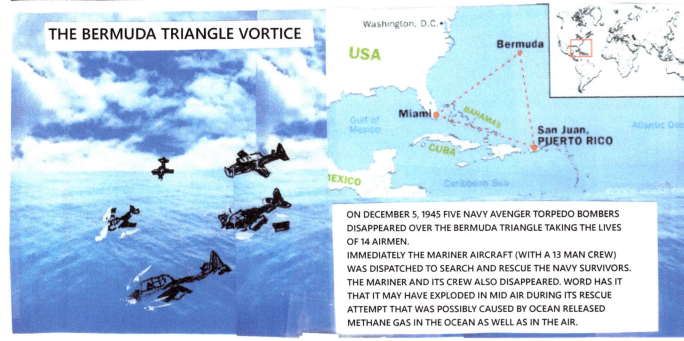

ON DECEMBER 5, 1945 FIVE NAVY AVENGER TORPEDO BOMBERS DISAPPEARED OVER THE BERMUDA TRIANGLE TAKING THE LIVES OF 14 AIRMEN.
IMMEDIATELY THE MARINER AIRCRAFT (WITH A 13 MAN CREW) WAS DISPATCHED TO SEARCH AND RESCUE THE NAVY SURVIVORS. THE MARINER AND ITS CREW ALSO DISAPPEARED. WORD HAS IT THAT IT MAY HAVE EXPLODED IN MID AIR DURING ITS RESCUE ATTEMPT THAT WAS POSSIBLY CAUSED BY OCEAN RELEASED METHANE GAS IN THE OCEAN AS WELL AS IN THE AIR.

CONCLUSION

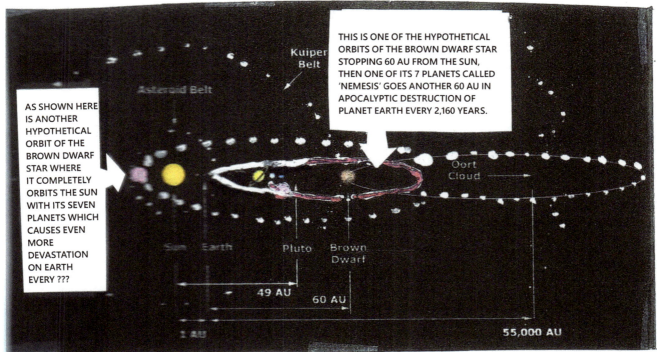

AS SHOWN HERE IS ANOTHER HYPOTHETICAL ORBIT OF THE BROWN DWARF STAR WHERE IT COMPLETELY ORBITS THE SUN WITH ITS SEVEN PLANETS WHICH CAUSES EVEN MORE DEVASTATION ON EARTH EVERY ???

THIS IS ONE OF THE HYPOTHETICAL ORBITS OF THE BROWN DWARF STAR STOPPING 60 AU FROM THE SUN, THEN ONE OF ITS 7 PLANETS CALLED 'NEMESIS' GOES ANOTHER 60 AU IN APOCALYPTIC DESTRUCTION OF PLANET EARTH EVERY 2,160 YEARS.

SCIENTISTS ESTIMATE THAT THE BROWN DWARF STAR, BDS, ALSO CALLED PLANET X IS 95,000 AU FROM THE SUN --- SLIGHTLY BEYOND THE OORT CLOUD.
HOWEVER, THE BDS IS STILL WITHIN THE GRAVITATIONAL PULL OF THE SUN. EVERY 2,200 YEARS THE BDS MIGHT COME WITHIN ??? FROM THE SUN, AND ONE OF ITS SEVEN ORBITING PLANETS, NEMESIS, TRAVELS ANOTHER 60 AU TOWARD THE SUN AND CAN CAUSE APOCALYPTIC DESTRUCTION TO EARTH

SOME ASTRONOMERS SAY THE BROWN DWARF STAR, BDS, (ALSO CALLED PLANETS X) HAS SEVEN PLANETS THAT ORBIT IT, AND IF THE BDS DOES COMPLETELY ORBIT THE SUN EVERY 2,160 YEARS, THEN IT WILL POLARIZE PLANET EARTH WHEREBY THE VARIOUS CONTINENTS (WHICH ARE RESTING PON MAGNA) WILL SWISH AROUND CAUSING MASSIVE DESTRUCTION OF LAND, SEA AND THE PEOPLE ON EARTH. THE ELLYPTICAL ORBIT OF THE BDS WILL UPEND AND DESTROY ANYTHING WITHIN 67 AU OF IT.

OUR EARTH SPINS ON ITS AXIS 1,040 MPH AT A 23.4% ANGLE. EARTH ORBITS THE SUN AT A SPEED OF 66,000 MPH WHILE TRAVELLING THROUGH THE ZODIAC.

THE EARTH IS 1 AU AWAY FROM THE SUN. ONE AU EQUALS 93 MILLIONS MILES.

THE SUN SPINS ON ITS AXIS 4,000 MPH AND TRAVELS THROUGH THE CORE OF OUR MILKY WAY GALAXY AT A SPEED OF 450,000 MPH. IT TAKE THE SUN 250 MILLION YEARS TO ORBIT THE CORE OF THE MILKY WAY.

OUR SOLAR SYSTEM IS LOCATION IN THE ORION ARM OF THE MILKY WAY. THE MILKY WAY GALAXY IS 100,000 LIGHT YEARS WIDE. ONE LIGHT YEAR, ROUNDED OFF, IS EQUAL TO ABOUT 6 TRILLION MILES.

THERE ARE BILLIONS OF SUN LIKE OURS IN THE MILKY WAY GALAXY. SOME BIGGER AND SOME SMALLER. SOME SUNS UN THE UNIVERSE ARE 1,000 TIMES LARGER THAN THE SUN IN OUR SOLAR SYSTEM.

OUR SOLAR SYSTEM IN THE ORION ARM OF THE MILKY WAY IS 30,000 LIGHT YEARS FROM THE INFAMOUS BLACK HOLE

THERE ARE MANY SCIENTISTS, GOVERNMENT OFFICIALS, WORLD LEADERS AS WELL AS CLERICAL WHO BELIEVE THAT THE UFOS ARE CAPTAINED BY SPACE ALIENS.

BUT THEIR ASSUMPTIONS ARE DEAD WRONG AS THE ALLEGED SPACE ALIENS ARE NOTHING MORE THAN SATAN'S DEMONS POSED AS SPACE ALIIENS.

SATAN AND 1/3RD OF THE ANGELIC DEMONS WERE CAST OUT OF HEAVEN AND ONTO EARTH.

THEY ARE POSING AS SPACE ALIENS IN ORDER TO SET UP SATAN'S ONE-WORLD ORDER GOVERNMENT.

SATAN WILL CREATE MANY FANTASTIC AND MYSTICAL OCCURRENCES IN THE SKY TO DECEIVE MANY INTO BELIEVING HE IS THE LORD.

OUR MILKY WAY TRAVELS THROUGH THE UNINVERSE AT A SPEED OF 1.4 MILLION MPH. AND THE VARIOUS GALAXIES LIKE OUR MILKY WAY ARE HELD TOGETHER BY BLACK MATTER AND ALSO SEPARATED BY IT.

THE LORD GOD IN JOB 26:7 STATED, "I CREATED THE EARTH SUSPENDED ON NOTHING."
AND IN GENESIS 1:18, GOD SAID, "I ALSO MADE THE STARS IN THE UNIVERSE."

OUR GOVERNMENT AND GOVERNMENTS AROUND THE WORLD ARE BUILDING UNDER-GROUND BUNKERS TO ALLEGEDLY PREPARE FOR AN APOCALYPTIC EVENT --- POSSIBLY LIKE PLANET X.

BUT LITTLE DO THEY REALIZE THAT IT IS ALL IN VAIN AS THOSE BUNKERS WILL BE FLOODED, CAVE IN, AND ALREADY HAVE FUNGAI, PARASITES AND OTHER DISEASES IN THEM.

BUT FEAR NOT, YOU WHO ARE "BORN AGAIN" BELIEVERS IN HAVING CHRIST AS YOUR LORD, KING, AND SAVIOR.

FOR WITH A BLAST OF THE ANGEL'S TRUMPETS, THE HOLY SPIRIT OF GOD WILL RAPTURE ALL WHO BELIEVE IN CHRIST UP INTO HEAVEN TO MEET JESUS --- BEFORE THE END-TIME APOCALYPSE BEGINS.

YES, INDEED, JESUS IS COMING SOON!

*******References*******

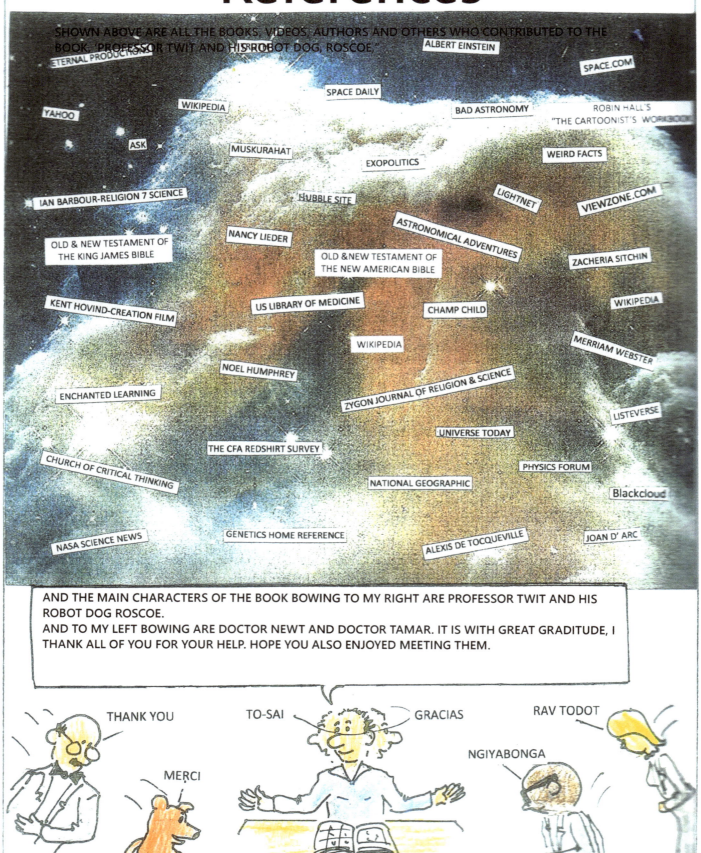

A PERSONAL THANK YOU TO THE WORLD-WIDE READERS AND SOME OF THEIR MANY LANGUAGES.

You must decide for yourself --- just what is Science, Religion, Fact or Fiction. But be sure you are sure.

For all books are made for you to <u>accept</u>, <u>reject</u> or <u>modify</u> to your way of thinking and living.

Acknowledgement

First and foremost, I want to thank the Good Lord, Jesus Christ, His Holy Spirit, His Spirit of Wisdom, His Angels and Archangels --- all in honor and glory of Father God Yahweh.

Secondly and also very, very importantly is my wife, Gail, who helps and guides me in many ways ... along with my family members who contribute in so many ways, also.

Third is my thanks to the following people who have reviewed, edited, and added to this book; namely --- See page 116.

And fourth, but as important as anyone, are the various authors, people and other organizations from whom I have gained access to important data pertaining to this book.

My thanks goes out to all the above, for I am but an Appointed Scribe and nothing more.

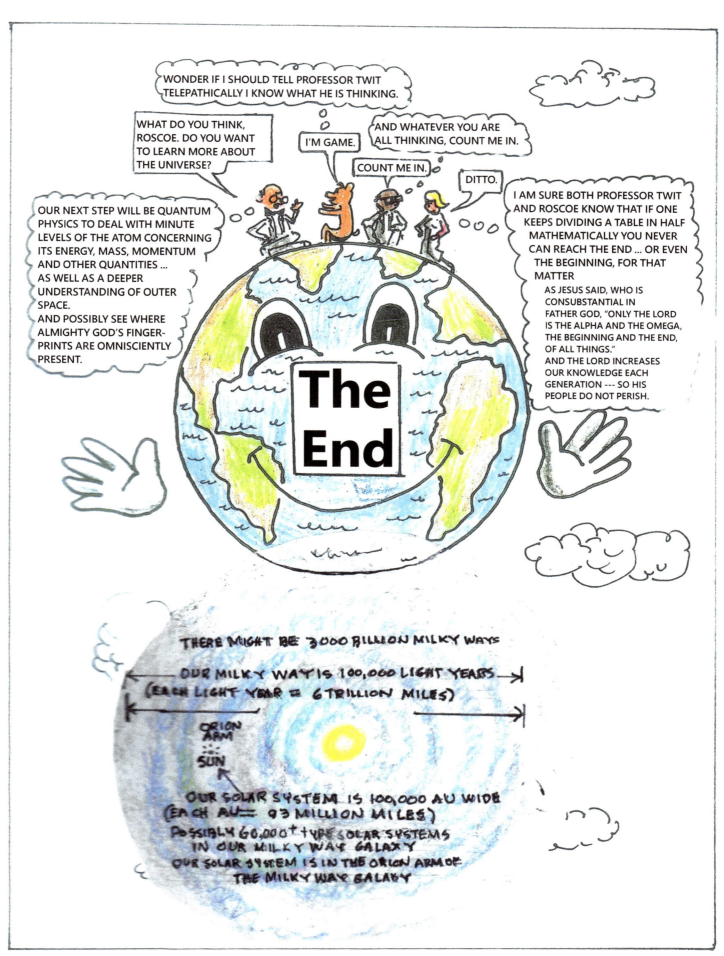

A special thanks to my lovely wife, Gail, who always sacrifices for me and the family. And to my beloved family members (also friends and relatives) who have played an instrumental part in our life --- due to the love, nurturing and care of my wife.

It is also imperative to know that neither myself, nor any other member of my family members are not without fault. Like other families, we spiritually dust ourselves off in Jesus' Mercy (undeserved forgiveness) and His Grace (unmerited favor) and continue on life's eventual journey to Heaven.

In conclusion, I want to thank Father God Yahweh, His only begotten Son, Jesus Christ, (my Lord, King and Savior), the Holy Spirit, the Spirit of Wisdom --- and the intercessory prayers of the Angels, Archangels, Apostles, Martyrs, Prophets and Saints to the Lord God, on my behalf, to complete this book.

And a special thanks to the contributors of this book namely: Gail Warren, Bill Warren, Kim Warren, Lisa and Wayne Dollard, Renee Russell and Jim Bodnar Joe Buresch, Doug Ettinger, Pastor Bill Roemer, Professor Brendon LaBuz, Professor Laniko Ruznitskaya, Pastors Keith and Linn Eggert, and (if I forgot anyone) your reward by father God will far exceed your name being listed here ... and a very special thanks to the tireless editing of my grandson. Michael Russell and a special thanks to Pastor Dick Diamond who creased "Bible Walk in Mansfield Ohio.

HOW THE LORD GOD COMMUNICATES WITH US.

The Lord God's Spirit can communicate with us via TV, movie, scripture, music, spiritual mentor, church, nature animals (remember that the donkey spoke to Balaam) or a host of other ways. In many instances the Holy Spirit of God speaks to us in our subconscious as we are sleep, or He might even interrupt your conscious brain waves if something very important, dangerous or needs to be immediately rectified. For now, let's laser on how the Lord God's Spirit utilizes our BRAIN WAVES when prompting us with an urgent or important message.

In the Book of Numbers 22:28 we read where the Lord's Spirit had a donkey speak to Balaam. Yes, the Lord can even speak to us via a donkey, so He is virtually unlimited in the ways and manners He can convey His thoughts to us.

The Lord God spoke directly to Adam, Cain, Noah, Moses and Samuel to name a few. The Lord God also spoke to John the Baptist when He said, "This is My beloved Son, in whom I am well pleased."

So, in essence, we are a walking telephone pole. Our brain operates via digital and analog electronic cycles connected to our brain waves of Alpha, Beta, Theta, Delta and Gamma Brain Waves that, in turn, work harmoniously with our GUT, IMMUNE SYSTEM and NERVE ENDINGS. Resultantly, the Lord God knows not only what you are doing, but also even with what you are thinking. Oh, yeah. For **thoughts** eventually turn into **words**, and **words** ultimately become our very **good or bad deeds.**

Now the Devil also can tap into your electronic system. But the Good Lord also knows what is in your very heart, which the Devil cannot begin to know or understand.

If you are thinking evil <u>thoughts</u>, bad words and committing <u>criminal</u> deeds, then the Devil has already entered your brain waves --- or he is about to guide you into something very sinful or dangerous to your safety.

Some inner sources say that the aliens (who are really demons) have contact with the military in Nevada Area 51. They have allegedly convinced the military to exchange technological advances in exchange for humans on the pretense that the aliens (again who are demons) will experiment on the humans to extend our life span. Not good. Not good at all. A total lie.

The demons string the humans out and their inner parts (gut, brain, nerve endings, etc) are wired to understand how, when, where, why, what and if we are thinking to detect who might be capable of betraying Satan. Worry not, though, as Satanic forces can never begin to decipher how the Lord God communicates with His "born again" believers. God's level of communications with us can never be broken or understood by Satanic forces.

Satan studies the Bible night and day to even try to understand it --- as well as the Lord's people. But it is all in vain, for the Omnipotent, Omnificent, Omniscient, and Omnipresent intellect of the Lord God is supernatural and He and only He contains its eternal knowledge.

> OUR BRAIN WAVES COMMUNICATE WITH THE GUT AND AUTOIMMUNE SYSTEM AS WELL AS WITH OUR NEVER ENDINGS. THE IMMUNE SYSTEM AND THE GUT CAN ACCEPT OR REJECT OR RELAY AN ALTERNATE MESSAGE FOR THE BRAIN WAVES TO ACCEPT, REJECT OR MODIFY. IT IS A GOD TWO-WAY-BUILT-IN-SYSTEM TO BEST SERVE OUR NEEDS FOR A MORE HEALTHY LIFE.

LET NOT THE EVIL ONE ENTICE OR OBSTRUCT THE WORD OF GOD.

Good. You followed the three basic steps to be spiritually "born again.' Yes, you were born physically and had a physical dad and mother. Some of you come from broken families, but dread not, as your true father is Father God, your true brother is Christ Jesus, and your true mother is Mother Mary.

The three steps to be "born again" are (1) <u>Repent</u>, which is more than sorry; it means you intend to change your life style. You will never be perfect, but you now have Jesus MERCY (undeserved forgiveness) and His GRACE (unmerited favor). But do not go back (backslide) into previous sinful situations. (2) Accept Jesus as your Lord and Savior (the Jews now call Him Yeshua.) (3) Ask for the Holy Spirit to enter your very being; as it was the Holy Spirit of God that raised Jesus from the dead, and He is the same Holy Spirit who will rapture you out of hell's fire and brimstone into the glorious abode of heaven ... that eye has not seen or ear has heard of its wonderful place of splendid eminence with a special purposeful position in which you will eternally perform along with a beautiful home.

Now please bear in mind that Satan will strive to prevent you from being "born again." This is what the Book of Matthew 13:4-9 states where some seed fell on the ground and the birds devoured them." Jesus explained to the disciples that is where and when Satan steals the word of God from the newly Christian believer.

Some of the seed (words of God) fell on a stony place where they could not take deep root and the Sun scorched and withered them away. Jesus defined that as a person who is filled with great joy, but when Satan brought forth tribulation and earthly torment upon the believer, he stumbles and departs from the truth of God's word.

And some of the seed fell among the thorns and bushes which chocked them." Jesus conveys to the disciples that the riches and deceitfulness of the world choke the word and the believer becomes unfruitful.

But other seed falls on the good ground and yields a crop of hundreds of fold abundance with some more and some less, but all fruitful and rewarded. Jesus further explained where the tares grow with the wheat; but at the End Time, He will say to the reapers, "Gather the tares in bundles and burn them, but gather the wheat and place it in My barn."

Also, always bear in mind, that <u>temptation</u> is not a sin ... it is, instead, a test of your <u>resolve</u> to stay well within the word of God.

So, beware of the Evil One who scours the face of the Earth to discourage and steal away your spiritual passport seed into Heaven. The Devil is filled with lies of obstruction and accusation. Satan can give you a thousand excuses for committing a sin, and not even one is valid in the eyes of the Lord God.

Go now and let not the Evil One steal your spiritually "born again" passport into Heaven. Ask that God's Holy Spirit, His Spirit of Wisdom, His Angels and Arch Angels and His intercession of apostles, saints, prophets and martyrs help release your from a hostage of Satan to the paid ransom of Jesus' blood.

Brief Chronology of God's Creation of The World.

3-8-15 Bill Warren

(1) When God created Adam from the dust of the ground, He later produced Eve from Adam's rib. There was some disturbance in heaven when the Lord decided to create mankind. But Father God had plans far beyond even the imagination of all who thought differently. Thus mankind was conceived.
Genesis 1:27

(2) God not only created the Earth, He created the entire universe. There are trillions of suns (some smaller and 1,000 times bigger than our sun). There are trillions of stars in our Milky Way Galaxy which is 100,000 light years wide --- and God knows each and every star by name.
Genesis 1:1, Job 26:7

(3) Father God said, "My angels will protect mankind from the elements." But Satan replied, "Not me. For ???an is far below my status in heaven."
???e arrogance and betrayal of Satan gathered one-
???d of the angels against God. A heavenly battle
???sued and God's Archangels and Angels tossed
???can and all his angels (demons) from heaven
???ing. "Woe unto you on earth. Beware for unto
??? comes the devil and all his lying, sinful ways."
Revelation 12:7-12

(4) The devil and his demons cohabitation with not only with the women on Earth (who produced giant children (some 50 feet tall) ... but to mock God further, the demons gave birth by commingling with the birds, beasts and reptiles. Seeing all this, God had Noah build the Noah's Ark to flood the Earth and rid the Earth of all the giant humans, animals and the sinful, unrighteous people.
Genesis 6:1-8

(5) Some of the demonic giants were as huge as the prehistoric dinosaurs. The giants had the men and women feed them from their livestock and crops. But the people could not keep up with the voracious appetite of the giants, so the giants began eating the people. Again, this made the Lord God flood the Earth to get rid of the giants According to 2 peter: 3-10 as mankind falls away from the precepts of Almighty God (as is evident today) then a great fire will destroy the Earth.

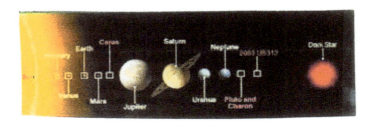

(6) The Third Trumpet in the Book of revelation proclaims that the "Wormwood" Star will fall on Earth polluting all the drinking water and scourging the Earth killing one-third of mankind. There is allegedly a Brown Dwarf Star in our Solar System that might contain the Wormwood Star. Some call it Nibiru, Nemesis as well as other synonymous names. Scientists, astronomers and theologians say, "It is not a matter of 'if' but 'when' the End Time comes to Earth.
Revelation 8:10-11

(7)

6,000+ Years Since God Created Mankind Signals The End Times.

	2344 BC	1446 BC	597 BC	29 AD	2000 AD
God Creates Mankind	Noah's Flood	Exodus of Israel from Egypt	Jerusalem Destroyed	Advent of Jesus	Last Days Begin

⟵ – – – – – 6000+ Years ... Time Is Drawing Nigh! – – – – ⟶

(8) Jesus said, "Verily, verily I say unto you except a person be 'born again' they cannot enter the Kingdom of God." (John 3: 3).
You are born the first time by a physical parent. Your second birth is when you are born spiritually by repenting of all your sins and accepting Jesus as your Lord, King and Savior.
Then the Holy Spirit, who raised Jesus from the dead, will enter you and raise you up to heaven during the "rapture" to meet Jesus in the sky above.
Jesus' shed blood for your sins provides you with His "Mercy" (undeserved forgiveness) and His "Grace" (unmerited favor) when you repent and accept Him.

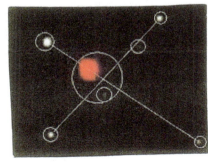

(9) The coming Nibiru "Cross" in the sky which consists of Nibiru and its moons --- has the Illuminists spending trillions of dollars for telescopes and underground bunkers. All of this is to no avail, for only the "born again" Judeo/Christians will be saved and raptured into heaven.

(10) The "Wormwood" Star is sometimes referred to as Nibiru, Hercolumbus, Nemesis or other names. It depends not on its speed, size or other descriptions. What determines its final collision with Earth is when mankind totally separates themselves from the precepts of Almighty God and accept not His only begotten Son, Jesus Christ. Matthew 24:3-51

(11) Underground bunkers have been built in the United States. One of the biggest is under to the Denver International Airport. Countries around the world are building underground bunkers which cost trillions of dollars. Question is --- are they a defense for nuclear attack, flu epidemic or the Earth's collision with the "Wormwood" Star which may be one of the seven planets orbiting the Brown Dwarf Star --- the Binary Sun of our Solar System.

(12) There will be a final battle at Armageddon where Almighty God and Jesus Christ (with His Archangels and Angels) defeat Satan, the Beast and the Antichrist and tosses them into the pit of fire and sulfur, Revelation 20:10

(13) Jesus Christ then decides who will be in the "Book of Life" or the dreaded "Book of Death". Revelation 20:15

Shemitah --- a time (seven year cycle) when God designates that the land be laid fallow and debts forgiven.

> ROSCOE, AS YOU WELL KNOW, GOD NOT ONLY HAS AN END-TIME CYCLE ... BUT ALSO A SEVEN YEAR CYCLE CALLED A SHEMITAH. THIS IS WHERE GOD BRINGS A REWARD OF A NEMISES TO A NATION AND ITS PEOPLE.

> RIGHT YOU ARE PROFESSOR TWIT. THE SHEMITAH COMES EVERY SEVEN YEARS RIGHT ON THE DAY, HOUR, MINUTE AND EXACT SECOND WITH GOD'S PRIZE OR RETRIBUTION TO EACH NATION AND IT'S PEOPLE.

> *PENDING ON THAT NATION'S BEHAVIOR.*

> AS YOU ALSO KNOW, THE BIBLE BEGINS WITH GOD'S CREATION OF THE WORLD. THIS SIGNIFIES HIS ENTIRE OWNERSHIP OF THE EARTH AND THE ENTIRE WORLD. HE ALONE PRODUCES GOOD OR BAD RESULTS PENDING ON A NATIONS ADHERENCE TO HIS PRECEPTS.

> YES AND SHEMITAH IS ONLY ONE OF 613 LAWS OF GOD. BUT THE SHEMITAH BRINGS GOD'S REWARD OR TROUBLE EVERY SEVEN YEARS --- WITHOUT FAIL. A TIME WHEN THE LAND IS TO BE FALLOW AND DEBTS ARE TO BE LIBERATED,

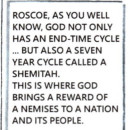

> SHEMITAH IS A TIME WHEN GOD SHOWS HE ALONE PRODUCES THE CROPS, MONIES, AND THE NECESSARY NEEDS OF A NATION --- JUST AS HE DID FOR THE ISRAELITES DURING THEN EXODUS THEN THROUGH AND TO THE PROMISED LAND.

> THE SEVENTH YEAR REST OF THE LAND PROVES THAT GOD STILL PROVIDES THE NEEDS AND NECESSITIES OF THE PEOPLE EVEN WHEN THE LAND LIES FALLOW AND DEBTS ARE FORGIVEN. AND ALSO IMPORTANT IS HIS REWARD OR PUNISHMENT UPON INDIVIDUAL NATIONS.

> ONE ONLY HAS TO REVIEW THE LAST 40 YEARS IN THE UNITED STATES OF AMERICA ECONOMY WHERE THE YEARS 1973, 1980, 1987, 2001 AND 2008 WERE ECONOMIC COLLAPSES. ONCE AGAIN PROVING THE VALIDITY OF GOD'S SEVEN YEAR CYCLE OF THE SHEMITAH'S GOOD OR BAD REWARD. ONE CAN LOOK INTO A MIRROR TO SEE HIS SHEMITAH FATE.

> NOW ONE WONDERS JUST WHAT MIGHT HAPPEN BY SEPTEMBER 28, 2022 TO THE VARIOUS NATIONS PENDING ON THEIR RIGHTEOUSNESS DURING THE PAST SEVEN YEARS.

> YEAH, LIKE MIRROR MIRROR, ON THE ON THE WALL, HOPE I DO NOT FALL.

The Four Jewish Holy Day Blood Moon and Two Solar Eclipses in 2014 & 2015

> SHOWN HERE, ROSCOE, ARE TWO SOLAR AND FOUR LUNAR ECLIPSES WHICH HAVE OCCURRED ON JEWISH HOLY DAYS. AND NO OTHER SOLAR OR LUNAR ECLIPSES HAVE OCCURRED DURING THIS TIME PERIOD. SOMETHING BIG IS GOING TO HAPPEN IN SEPTEMBER 2022

| 15 April 2024 Jewish Passover Eclipse | 8 Oct 2014 Feast of Tabernacle Eclipse | 20 March 2015 Jewish New Years for Kings Eclipse | 4 April 2015 Jewish Passover Eclipse | 13 Sept 2015 Feast of Trumpets Eclipse | 28 Sept 2015 Feast of Tabernacle Eclipse |

THE SEVEN JEWISH HOLY DAYS ARE:

1. PASSOVER
2. UNLEAVENED BREAD
3. FIRST FRUITS
4. PENECOST
5. TRUMPHETS (ROSH HASHANAH)
6. ATONEMENT (YOM KIPPUR)
7. TABERNACLES

AND HANUKKAH IS ALSO CELEBRATED

HOW JEWISH AND CHRISTIAN HOLY DAYS COINCIDE IN 2015

JEWISH HOLY DAY	DATE	CELEBRATION	CHRISTIAN HOLY DAY	CELEBRATION
PASSOVER	4-3-15	Lamb's blood set them free	JESUS ON THE CROSS	Jesus' shed blood salvation.
UNLEAVENED BREAD	4-4-15	No leaven (sin) in eaten bread	JESUS DIED WITHOUT SIN	Jesus is the epitome of no sin.
FIRST FRUITS	4-5-15	First crops offered to God	JESUS IS THE FIRST FRUIT	Jesus is the First Fruit from dead.
PENTECOST	7-31-15	The Law Fifty days after Passover	JESUS OVERCOMES THE LAW	Apostles meet 50 days after Passover
ROSH HASHANAH	9-15-15	Jews celebrate New Year	JESUS BEGINS HIS REIGN	Jesus amidst trumpets appears.
YOM KIPPUR	9-23-15	Atonement for past sins	JESUS' ATONES FOR ALL SIN	Jesus mercy & grace atones all sin.
TABERNACLES	12-7-15	Jews build small tabernacles	JESUS IS THE ETERNAL ARK	Jesus is the eternal Tabernacle/

ANOTHER JEWISH HOLIDAY IS HANUKKAH: (December 7, 2015) in which the candle flame (light) kept burning. The Christians celebrate Christmas (December 25, 2015) as Jesus is the "Eternal Light."   The book life and death will be read someday between Rosh Hashanah and Yom kippur.

> **Scientists, theologians, astronomers, thought leaders and others say, "The End Time is not a matter of 'if' But 'when.'" And every seven years the Lord God emits the "Shemitah" rewarding or punishing nations.**

(1) THE BIBLE WAS WRITTEN ABOUT 1,500 YEARS AGO. AND JESUS FULFILLED ALL OF THE PROPHECIES IN ORDER OF THEIR TIME AND SEQUENCE:
Read William Loyal Warren ts, "48 Prophecies of God About His Only Begotten Son Jesus Christ." Actually, Jesus fulfilled hundreds of prophecies and many more than one's mind can imagine 104

(2) THE BIBLE HAS BEEN WRITTEN BY 40 DIFFERENT WRITERS. IN THREE DIFFERENT LANGUAGES, OVER THREE DIFFERENT CONTINENETS DURING THAT 1,500 YEAR TIME PERIOD:
If the Lord God does not intervene, the Devil will deceive the people/ 104

(3) HOW JEWISH AND CHRISTIAN HOLIDAYS COINCIDE IN 2015:

JEWISH HOLY DAY	DATE	CELEBRATION	CHRISTIAN HOLY DAY	CELEBRATION
PASSOVER	4-3-15	Lamb's blood set them free	JESUS ON THE CROSS	Jesus' shed blood salvation.
UNLEAVENED BREAD	4-4-15	No leaven (sin) in eaten bread	JESUS DIED WITHOUT SIN	Jesus is the epitome of no sin.
FIRST FRUITS	4-5-15	First crops offered to God	JESUS IS THE FIRST FRUIT	Jesus is the First Fruit from dead.
PENTECOST	7-31-15	The Law Fifty days after Passover	JESUS OVERCOMES THE LAW	Apostles meet 50 days after Passover
ROSH HASHANAH	9-16-15	Jews celebrate New Year	JESUS BEGINS HIS REIGN	Jesus amidst trumpets appears.
YOM KIPPUR	9-23-15	Atonement for past sins	JESUS' ATONES FOR ALL SIN	Jesus mercy & grace atones all sin.
TABERNACLES	12-7-15	Jews build small tabernacles	JESUS IS THE ETERNAL ARK	Jesus is the eternal Tabernacle/

.... 105

(4) THE 12 VORTICES AROUND THE GLOBE CAUSE MANY SHIPS TO LOSE THEIR BUOYANCY AND SINK FROM (UNDER THE SEA) RISING VOLCANO METHANE --- AND EVEN PILOTS IN PLANES GET OVERCOME BY THE METHANE AND BECOME CONFUSE AND BEFUDDLED AND CRASH.
The 12 Vortices are where most of the ships and planes have sunk or crash from the methane 106

(5) TEN OF THE VORTICES ARE LOCATED IN THE EARTH'S TROPICAL CLIMATE, AND ONE IS LOCATED IN THE NORTH POLES AND ONE IN THE SOUTH POLE:
The Bermuda Triangle Vortice is the best known one 107

(127)

(6) **PROFESSOR JOSEPH MONAGAHAN AND HIS HONOR STUDENT, DAVID MAY, OF MONASH UNIVERSITY IN AUSTRALIA UNCOVERED THAT THE METHANE GAS BUBBLES CAUSE SHIPS TO LOSE THEIR BUOYANCY AND SINK AND THE INHALING OF THE GAS BUBBLED CAUSE PILOTS TO LOSE CONSCIOUSNESS AND CRASH.**
Thus, you can now understand why and how ships sink and planes crash around the various 12 Vortices 108

(7) **IN 1947, PRESIDENT HARRY TRUMAN HAD SEC. OF DEFENSE, JAMES FORESTAL COMMISSION ADMIRAL BYRD TO EXAMINE THE SOUTH POLE VORTICE:**
While investigating the South Pole Vortice, Admiral Byrd and his fleet of 40 ships and 1,400 sailors were attacked by UFO type aircrafts and he retreated back to America as he said, "If I did not, I would lose his entire fleet." 109

(8) **BESIDES OUR BASIC 5 SENSES OF HEARING, SEEING, TASTING, SMELLING, AND TOUCHING, WE ALSO HAVE THE EXTRA SENSE OF "INSTINCT:**
Animals basically work off their instinct in knowing various aspects of migration etc 110

All US PRESIDENTS 9BASED ON GENEALOGICAL STUDY ARE RELATED TO KING JOHN LACKLAND PLANTAGANET WITH THE EXCEPTION OF MARTIN VAN BUREN AND DONALD TRUMP:
King John Lackland Plantaganet was the son of King Henry11 who was married to an Isralelite, Eleanor of Aquitaine... 110

(10) **THE BIBLE IS THE BOOK THAT EXCEEDS THE NUMBER OF COPIES THAT THAT HAVE BEEN PRINTED IN THAT 5,600 WERE MADE OF IT SINCE 50 TO 100 YEARS. WHEREAS ONLY 7 COPIES WERE MADE OF PLATO, 10 COPIES WERE MADE OF CAESAR. 49 COPIES WERE MADE OF ARISTOTLE, 643 COPIES WERE MADE OF HOMER;S ILIAD, SO THE BIBLE, FAR AND AWAY, IS THE MOST AUTHENTICATED BOOK**
The above ist of books authenticate that the Bible is the most valid sourse of written proof 111

IN ORDER TO AUTHENTICATE THE BIBLE, ONE HAS TO DETERMINE WHEN THE ORIGINAL WAS WRITTEN AND THE APPROXIMATE TIME SPAN BETWEEN THE ORIGINAL AND ANY COPIES MADE OF IT.

FOR EXAMPLE, **PLATO'S** ORIGINAL WAS WRITTEN 427-327 B.C. AND 1,200 YEARS IS THE TIME SPAN WHEN 7 COPIES WERE MADE OF IT.

CAESAR'S ORIGINAL WAS WRITTEN 100-44 B.C. AND 1,200 YEARS IS THE TIME SPAN WHEN 10 COPIES WERE MADE OF IT.

ARISTOTLE'S ORIGINAL WAS WRITTEN 384-322 B.C. AND 1,400 YEARS IS THE TIME SPAN WHEN 49 COPIES WERE MADE OF IT.

HOMER'S ILIAD ORIGINAL WAS WRITTEN 900 B.C. AND 500 YEARS IS THE TIME SPAN WHEN 643 COPIES WERE MADE OF IT.

AND THE **NEW TESTAMENT** OF THE BIBLE'S ORIGINAL WAS WRITTEN 50-100 A.D. AND 100 YEARS IS THE TIME SPAN WHEN 5,600 COPIES WERE MADE OF IT.

SO YOU CAN SEE WHERE THE BIBLE IS THE MOST AUTHENTICATED BOOK OF THE ABOVE LISTED AUTHORS.

(11) **SOME OF PLATO'S EPIC SAYINGS:**

We can only forgive a child who is afraid of the dark. The real tragedy of life is when men are afraid of the Light

The price one pays for indifference to public indoctrination is to be ruled by evil people. Plato was described as a Christian in belief. Seven copies were written of this book.

CAESAR'S DICTUM'S (49 -44 BC)
One of Caesar's famous quotes is, "I came, I saw and I conquered. Only 10 copies are produce of it.

Caesar was 52 years old when he and the 21 year old Cleopatra entered into a love affair. They had a child named Ptolemy Caesar. Ten copies are found of this book.

The book titles, "The 12 Caesars" was written by Suetonius that details the ki9nd f reign of each Roman Emperor.

ARISTOTLE'S ORIGINAL WRITINGS:
Aristotle's teacher was Plato who was a student of Socrates. Many believe that Aristotle was one of the greatest philosophers and scientist. Just 49 Copies of it.

Aristotle's most famous student was Alexander The Great who he taught him for three years.

HOMER'S ILIAD WAS WRITTEN IN 900 BC;
The "Iliad" expresses the the best and worst aspects of Humankind, that encompass the reality and illusions of love, honor and the lustful force of power, sorrow and patriotism. A total of 643 copies were made of it.

A brief synopses of Homer's Iliad is an epic tale of the final days when Greece invades Troy and the intrigue, betrayals and quarrels between God and men as they war

THE NEW TESTAMENT OF THE BIBLE WAS 50-100 AD. AND 100 YEARS IS THE TIME SPAN WHEN 5,600 COPIES WERE MADE OF IT.
The Bible, then, is the most authenticated book of time and accuracy. It is the very words manifested by God..........112

(129)

(11) SOME OF PLUTO'S EPIC SAYINGS:

We can only forgive a child who is afraid of the dark.
The real tragedy of life is when men are afraid of the Light

The price one pays for indifference to public indoctrination is to be ruled by evil people. Plato was described as a Christian in belief. Seven copies were written of this book.

CAESAR'S DICTUM'S (49 -44 BC)
One of Caesar's famous quotes is, "I came, I saw and I conquered. Only 10 copies are produce of it.

Caesar was 52 years old when he and the 21 year old Cleopatra entered into a love affair. They had a child named Ptolemy Caesar. Ten copies are found of this book.

The book titles, "The 12 Caesars" was written by Suetonius that details the ki9nd f reign of each Roman Emperor.

ARISTOTLE'S ORIGINAL WRITINGS:
Aristotle's teacher was Plato who was a student of Socrates. Many believe that Aristotle was one of the greatest philosophers and scientist. Just 49 Copies of it.

Aristotle's most famous student was Alexander The Great who he taught him for three years.

HOMER'S ILIAD WAS WRITTEN IN 900 BC;
The "Iliad" expresses the the best and worst aspects of Humankind, that encompass the reality and illusions of love, honor and the lustful force of power, sorrow and patriotism. A total of 643 copies were made of it.

A brief synopses of Homer's Iliad is an epic tale of the final days when Greece invades Troy and the intrigue, betrayals and quarrels between God and men as they war

THE NEW TESTAMENT OF THE BIBLE WAS 50-100 AD. AND 100 YEARS IS THE TIME SPAN WHEN 5,600 COPIES WERE MADE OF IT.
The Bible, then, is the most authenticated book of time

and accuracy. It is the very words manifested by God……112

(12) **ALL THINGS WERE CREATED BY GOD BE THEY VISIBLE OR INVISIBLE--- BE THEY ARCH ANGELS, ANGELS OR WHATEVER; AS ALL THINGS WERE CREATED BY ALMIGHTY GOD:**
God made the Earth and it orbits the Sun at 66,000 MPH while spinning on its axis 1,040 MPH. The Earth is 93 million miles from the Sun, and it takes the Earth approximately 365 days to orbit the Sun. Our Solar System) travels through the core of the Milky Way Galaxy at a speed of 483,000 MPH. It takes our Sun (in our Solar System) 230 million years to orbit the inner core of our Milky Way Galaxy.. 113
Our Milky Way Galaxy travels through Space at a speed of 1.34 million MPH. It is estimated that there are 200 billion to 2 trillion galaxies in space. To try to study "eon" in time and numerically is practically impossible. So some things are just unfathomable.

(13) **IN JOB 27: 7, THE LORD, STATES, "I CREATED THE EARTH SUSPENDED ON NOTHING," AND IN GENESIS, THE LORD SAYS, "I ALSO CREATED THE STARS IN THE UNIVERSE."**
The UFO's are not piloted by Space Aliens, they are piloted by Demonic Entities who are striving to eventually have a One World Order on Earth for Satan to reign domain. Fear not, is the sound of the Angel's Trumpet, the Holy Spirit will capture all the "Born Again" believers into Heaven before the ???d Time Apocalypse 113

(14) **??? REFERENCES USED IN THE PRODUCTION OF THIS BOOK:**
Professor twit, Roscoe, Dr. Newt, and Dr. Tamar also thank all the contributors to this book ... 116

(15) **??? YOU, YOURSELF, WILL HAVE TO DECIDE WHETHER THIS BOOK IS --- FACT, FICTION, SCIENCE OR RELIGION ... OR MAYBE A LITLE ??? OF ALL THE ABOVE:**
??? assure you that I did not use any fiction in this book, ??? who knows for sure about anything, Only God knows 116

(17)	How the Lord communicates with us	117
	Don't be scared just get prepared by taking the three steps to be "Born Again" and Heaven sent	118
(18)	**FIRST ENDING CLOSE:** If one keeps cutting a table in half, theoretically, they will never get to the ending. Some astrologists say that there can be more than 3000 Billion Milky Way Galaxies. Our own Solar System is 100,000 AU wide (each AU equals 93 million miles) ... which is the distance of Earth from the Sun. Potentially there are around 60,000 of our type Solar Systems in our Milky Way Galaxy. Our Milky Way Galaxy is 100,000 Light Years wide ... every light year equals about 6 trillion miles. Our Solar System is presently in the Orion Arm of the Milky Way Galaxy. It the inner Our Solar System travels 515,000 MPH through theoretic inner core of our Milky Way Galaxy and it takes it 130 million years to orbit the inner core	119
(19)	**IS A PICTURE OF PROFESSOR TWIT, ROSCOE, DR. NEWT AND DR. TAMAR.** They are discussing the possibility of their story being published or being turned into a movie	119
(20)	**THE INVESTIGATION OF THE 13,000 YEAR BLACK KNIGHT SATELLITE.** The Black 10 tons Knight Satellite is around 70 feet in length and 30 feet in diameter. It weights about 10 tons and travels at the speed of light. It is not man-made, so what is it?	119
(21)	**A BRIE PICTORIAL CHRONOLOGY OF GOD'S CREATION OF THE WORLD.** * Adam & Eve, * Trillion of Galaxies, * Fallen Angesl, * Noah * Naphilim Giants, * Our Planets. *6,000 years of Earth. * Jesus; Crucifixion, * Nibiru Cross, * Wormwood Star, * Underground Bunkers, * Armageddon, * Book of Life & Death	120 121
(22)	**HOW JEWISH AND CHRISTIAN HOLIDAYS COINCIDE.** Shown below on page 123 are how Jewish and Christian Holidays coincide	122

Milton Keynes UK
Ingram Content Group UK Ltd.
UKHW052245141124
451207UK00016B/173